MW01168639

EVERY SAVAGE DESERVES A HOOD CHICK

J. DOMINQUE

Cole Hart

Every Savage Deserves A Hood Chick

Copyright © 2021 by J. Dominique

All rights reserved.

Published in the United States of America.

All rights reserved. No part of this publication may be reproduced, distributed, or transmitted in any form or by any means, including photocopying, recording, or other electronic or mechanical methods, without the prior written permission of the publisher, except in the case of brief quotations embodied in critical reviews and certain other noncommercial uses permitted by copyright law. For permission requests, please contact: www.colehartsignature.com

This is a work of fiction. Names, characters, places, and incidents either are the products of the author's imagination or are used fictitiously. Any resemblance of actual persons, living or dead, businesses, companies, events, or locales is entirely coincidental. The publisher does not have any control and does not assume any responsibility for author or third-party websites or their content.

The unauthorized reproduction or distribution of this copyrighted work is a crime punishable by law. No part of the book may be scanned, uploaded to or downloaded from file sharing sites, or distributed in any other way via the Internet or any other means, electronic, or print, without the publisher's permission. Criminal copyright infringement, including infringement without monetary gain, is investigated by the FBI and is punishable by up to five years in federal prison and a fine of $250,000 (www.fbi.gov/ipr/).

This book is licensed for your personal enjoyment only. Thank you for respecting the author's work.

Published by Cole Hart Signature, LLC.

Mailing List

To stay up to date on new releases, plus get information on contests, sneak peeks, and more,

Go To The Website Below...

www.colehartsignature.com

❧ I ❧

MAKIYAH

My music cutting off had my eyes snapping open, and I looked up just in time to see my dumb-ass baby daddy's back as he ventured towards our bedroom. Instantly the sadness I'd been wallowing in just a few seconds before disappeared, and in its place came immediate rage. This nigga had been gone all night, and was just now coming home like shit was supposed to be smooth. The fact that he didn't even speak, but just cut my music off and proceeded on his way really had me hot to the point that I didn't even see his friend Noah standing by the door. Struggling to stand up with my five-month pregnant belly, I finally got to my feet and stormed past him as he tried to stutter a hello. I was sure that he was already anticipating what was about to go down, but he knew his boy was wrong and if anything should've told him to bring his ass home. That would've been too much like right though with these niggas. Nobody held their friends accountable for their bullshit and instead just went with the flow even when they were blatantly living foul. At the end of the day, it wasn't Noah's responsibility to babysit Romell. As a grown-ass man with a kid and a pregnant girlfriend, he should have just known better.

By the time I made it to our bedroom, he was in the middle

of laying out clothes, as if he was going to be leaving right back out and that only pissed me off more. I know he heard the floor creak as I entered, but he didn't even lift his head out of our worn-down dresser to look my way.

"Uh, 'scuse you. Where the fuck you think you goin' Romell?" I finally asked when I realized that he wasn't going to acknowledge me at all. Even as mad as I was, I couldn't help but admire how fine he was as I stared upside his head with a look that could kill. I'd always liked my nigga's a little dark like me and tall, and Romell was all of the above. Standing at an even six feet, he was the color of peanut butte, covered in tattoos, and built very athletically. He kept his hair cut short with deep waves and his face clean-shaven, besides a small mustache and minimal chin hair. Just seeing his handsome face used to be enough to bring me out of the worst mood, but now it just made me want to punch the shit out of him.

Sighing like I was bothering him, he snatched a pair of boxers out of the drawer and slammed it back shut. "I need to go make some money." He said dryly, and I felt my frown deepen at the blatant lie.

"You're full of shit! Next you gon' tell me you was out making money last night too huh?"

"I'm not bouta do this shit with you Ma-." He started but I quickly cut him off.

"Not gon' do what? Explain yourself? I wouldn't even be able to stay out all night, let alone come waltzing up in here the next day like I don't got a nigga and without a good reason! On my soul I'm tired of this shit! If you don't want to be here then stay yo' ass away, it ain't like you do shit around here any mutha-fuckin' way!" He'd been focusing on the clothes he had laid out, but as soon as the last word left my mouth, his body went stiff, and he jerked his head in my direction.

"I don't do shit? What the fuck yo' ass do huh! You talkin' like you bringin' in something besides link and cash assistance!" he barked with his face twisted. "Fuck I'm comin' up in this bitch for? It ain't never no food here, it's dirty as hell and it ain't even like I can fuck you cause you barely wash yo' ass! I'll gladly leave this muhfucka! At least at Simone's crib, I know I can lay on some clean sheets next to a bitch that got something going for herself!" By now he was in my face, making sure I felt every piece of that insult, but none of what he'd said hurt me as bad as the comparison to the bitch I knew he was spending all of his time with. I was used to Romell using our circumstances against me and pretty much blaming me for how we were living. The thing was that he never took responsibility for what he did or lack thereof. Yes, at the moment I wasn't working and was living solely on Aid, but I was pregnant with *his* child and it wasn't like he would babysit for me to punch a clock. Sure, I didn't keep up with my hygiene or appearance, and I wasn't cleaning the house every time a dish was dirty, but I was depressed as hell behind his actions and his constant emotional and sometimes physical abuse. Most days it was hard as hell to even get out of bed to feed myself and our son RJ. He clearly didn't give a fuck about that though, because he was stuck so far up Simone's ass! At this point, he wasn't even trying to keep his dealings with her to himself, and not only was everybody aware of them being together he was working overtime to keep *me* a secret. I was out here pregnant and stuck with a toddler while he was out living his life like a single and childfree man.

It burned me up inside and made my already ill feelings worse, knowing that people looked at me like I was the side bitch when she was the one messing around with a nigga that already had a woman. Romell was a completely different nigga than the one I'd met almost five years ago. Gone was the kind and encouraging words, loyalty was foreign unless it was on my end and he damn sure hadn't kept any of his promises. I was convinced he'd trapped me with two kids just so he could keep me in his life and ensure no other man would want me. I should've been used to this though, or at the very least prepared, but I was almost positive that my loyalty would eventually pay off. Just thinking about how he was going to get off scot-free had me doing some shit I *never* would've even thought about doing before. I gathered up as much spit as I could and unloaded that shit right in his face, instantly wiping away the smug expression he was wearing. I didn't even give him a chance to react either. I just immediately started hitting him any and everywhere I could as obscenities flew from mouth. My tiny fists hardly had an effect on him though, and once his initial shock wore off, he snatched me up by my neck roughly.

This was usually the point where I would no longer put up a fight. Romell was much bigger and definitely stronger than me and no matter how mad I was the last thing I wanted was to push him to actually hit me. In the past the most he'd done was choke or bite me, saying that I was so little he couldn't bring himself to use that much force, but there'd been times like now when the look in his eyes showed that he could and would kill my ass. I'd surpassed my breaking point though, and was seeing red. Despite my oxygen supply being cut off, I was still punching, slapping and scratching at him.

"Bitch!" He shrieked when my nails dug into his eye causing him to simultaneously release his hold on my neck and push me away. Panting and slightly dizzy I fell backward over the small box fan we had cooling the sweltering room, but a mixture of anger and adrenaline had me right back on my feet. He was still holding his eye when I tossed that same fan at him and ran up for more. I was ready to get my payback in blood and had pretty much forgotten about my delicate state. There was just no way I could let him walk away freely after everything I'd gone through with him.

I'm not sure how long we actually tussled in that room, but it seemed like forever before I heard Noah's scary-ass at the door. "Aye, aye come on bro it ain't even worth it." He tried to reason and I instantly wanted to punch his ass too. I wasn't sure if he really felt like I wasn't worth it or if he was only trying to diffuse the situation, but I felt insulted as fuck. We were loud as hell bumping and crashing around and even though I was the aggressor Romell had me by about one hundred pounds, so it should've been obvious who the victim was to him. Fuck me being pregnant, and barely reaching this nigga's shoulder, his reasoning for stopping this shit was the fact that I wasn't worth it.

Almost as if Noah was his conscience Romell immediately pushed me off of him. "Sit the fuck down somewhere Makiyah before you fuck around and hurt the baby being stupid!" He ordered when he saw me gearing up to come at him again. Not trying to hear that shit I ran at him anyway, only for him to mush me back with much more force this time. "I said fuckin' stop!"

"Nigga fuck you!" Was my only response finally seeing that he may have meant business this time. Plus our brawl seemed to have awakened Rj and my cousin Dymani's baby, and their loud cries could be heard through the thin walls. Sneering, I pushed past him to tend to the kids and found them both standing right on the other side of the door. Like I often found myself doing I put on a smile as I knelt down and pulled them into a hug. "Hey hey, why y'all crying? I'm right here." I soothed glaring at Romell's stupid ass over their heads as he made his way out of our bedroom and right past us. The bum didn't even have the decency to speak to our crying baby, he was so thirsty to run back out to the streets. Sucking my teeth, I watched him and his flunky-ass friend until they disappeared out the door. If I didn't know it before I definitely knew now that he was undeserving of me and my tears, but that didn't stop me from crying right along with the kids.

❧ 2 ❧

DYMANI

"**O**n my soul this shit ain't never happened to me before." This nigga slurred and looked down at his limp ass dick in disbelief. For whatever reason he was still trying to get it to come to life even though I was well past turned off and definitely wouldn't fuck him if he was able to get it hard again. I felt played to be honest. Not only had I cut my night short, but I'd lost out on big tips to leave the club with his ass, and instead of breaking my three-month dry spell, I was sitting here just as sexually frustrated as ever. It served my ass right considering that I didn't know this nigga from a can of paint and had decided to fuck him just because he was fine as hell. I'd let my clit do the thinking for the first time in my life and ended up with a nigga with erectile dysfunction. No doubt if I told Makiyah this shit, she'd die laughing at my slow ass, so I was definitely going to keep it to myself. A bitch was just going to have to take this L and try to forget it even happened.

I was already scanning the room for my skimpy ass work uniform and plotting on how I'd make up for my lost wages when the sound of this nigga snoring had my head snapping back in his direction. My lip instantly curled at the sight of him knocked out with his hand still wrapped around that python he called a dick. It was a whole shame he was that blessed and couldn't even use it. I damn sure would've never guessed by looking at him. Just from the way he'd entered The Dollhouse looking like money and being shown the utmost respect, I knew he was that nigga. In addition to that every stripper in attendance turned the fuck up from his presence, which told me they all knew him to be a big spender. Usually, the way they were acting would've had me steering clear, but when I brought the array of bottles over to their section, even my hardcore ass got weak in the knees. Seeing him up close and personal hit different, and once his chocolate orbs took me in and he flashed me a sexy dimpled smile, I knew I was giving up the draws....well, at least I thought I was.

Resisting the urge to slap him awake, I stomped my mad ass around the room collecting my black boy shorts, the matching bikini top and my thigh-high black patent leather boots. I talked shit the entire time I got dressed but none of the noise I made caused that nigga to even flinch, irritating me more.

"I really can't believe this shit." I grumbled snatching up my purse from the desk they had in the hotel room. A bitch was so flabbergasted I couldn't even do shit once I was finished but stand there fuming and looking around as if I was lost until my eyes landed on his pants in the chair beside the bed. Instantly my mood perked up, and a slow grin spread across my face as I sashayed over.

Just as I'd expected he was like every other street nigga and carried all of his money around in thick knots. No wallet, no debit or credit cards just cash and weed, like he was in high school or some shit. Glancing over at his pathetic ass still in the same position I rolled my eyes and stuffed his money back into his pocket. Honestly, I would've been fully justified for taking out the amount I'd lost, but instead I simply took the ounce of weed I'd found. Just from the strong smell and hairs coming off it, I knew it was a really good grade, and after dealing with him I could definitely use a nice fat blunt.

Feeling somewhat vindicated, I made my way out of the room and to my car gaining a few knowing glances from the staff and random guests as I did. It probably looked to them like I was doing a walk of shame, but little did they know I was leaving that bitch with all my morals. I shot them hoes the same nasty look they were giving me and kept on about my business. Thankfully, I drove myself and didn't ride with his ass or I would've had to steal that nigga's car too. I hopped behind the wheel of my old Honda Civic and immediately wasted no time peeling out of the parking lot. I made sure to stop and grab a blunt already anticipating the hot bath I was about to soak in while I smoked.

Working at the club always left me with sore feet and tired arms in addition to an attitude from having to deal with a bunch of rude ass drunk niggas. The fact that I worked in a strip club and wore my little ass uniform had them feeling entitled to try and grab on me and make unwanted advances. I was a tough girl, and I could most definitely handle myself, but the shit was still draining though. It was never so bad that I'd quit because I made good money. In the six short months I'd been working there I was able to get me a car and a small two-bedroom for my baby and me. Being able to maintain both and still provide our necessities was more than enough to keep me going back every night.

Forty minutes later, I was pulling into an empty parking spot that wasn't too far away from my building which I was extremely thankful for. It was going on two in the morning and the last thing I wanted to do was walk blocks in what I had on. A bitch could never be too careful and as I locked my car up, I prepped the small knife and mace I always carried. The block was surprisingly dead for it to be Friday, but I wasn't complaining as I hurried to my buildings entrance and rushed into my first floor apartment. I didn't even realize I'd been holding my breath until the door locked behind me and I was able to release it.

"I see yo' ass still down there at that damn club."

I almost jumped out of my skin at the deep baritone, but recognition had me sucking my teeth as I flipped the light switch. My ex Twan didn't even flinch from the brightness as if his ass hadn't been sitting there in the dark like a psycho for God knows how long.

"No thanks to you!" I scoffed, unable to hide my disgust at the sight of him. I hadn't seen his ass in months, about three to be exact and I was positive that had been strategic on his part. At first, he'd been all for me working at the club, but after coming up there one night and witnessing the way niggas were lusting, he tried to make me quit. I rolled my eyes just thinking about him giving me an ultimatum to stop working there or else, like the nigga really said or else with his dramatic ass. That let me know right then that he really didn't give a fuck about us because who'd demand for me to quit my job without anything else in place. It was selfish if you asked me knowing that we were broke and living in his mama's house. Despite how he claimed to feel about my job, his ass was certainly enjoying the apartment and car I'd gotten with the money I made at first, but he made good on his promise and left my ass when I refused to quit. He even resorted to no longer keeping Armani for me while I worked and made sure his mama wouldn't either forcing me to ask Makiyah.

"You god damn right!" he hopped up, and I clenched my mace tighter. "How I look being cool with my bitch half-naked in front of a bunch of drunk niggas! Muhfuckas touchin' all on you and shit! Yo ass definitely wouldn't like it if it was the other way around and I was out here lettin' bitches touch on me for money!"

"I'm not bouta even go there with you *Antwan*, just give me my keys and gone on bout' your night." I dismissed everything he was saying because at this point it didn't matter. A nigga only had one chance to treat me funny and I was done with his ass, there was no back and forth with me. Instantly his forehead creased in defiance, and he closed the space between us. My horny ass couldn't help but take him in as the scent of his cologne hit me. Despite the hour he was dressed up in a plain white tee and some whitewashed, distressed Gucci jeans with brand new Retro Jordans on, probably having just left somebody's club. His dreads were freshly twisted and his line-up was crispy, letting me know that his ass had some type of money.

"You ain't gettin' shit back as long as Armani here I can come and go as I please." He said sounding dumb as hell.

"Oh, now you worried bout Armani?" I spat sarcastically. "We ain't seen yo' ass in months and you just now poppin' up like you daddy of the year-."

"I been workin'." He cut me off pulling out a stack of money that rivaled the shit I saw at the club every night, but I could tell it was more than dollar bills. "I been gone tryna stack this money so yo' ass can quit that bullshit ass job." His chest puffed out a little bit more as he flipped through the bills thinking that he had me. I will admit I wasn't expecting for him to flash a bunch of blue faces at me as an incentive to leave my job. As much as I loved him, the truth was Antwan was a fuck up. There was always a get rich quick scheme he had going on that never amounted to shit. I'd heard it all, from a rap career to credit card scams, and in the end, we ended up right back where we started and sometimes s worse off. So to see him with the amount of money he was currently holding had me suspicious as hell and my eyes narrowed into slits.

"Workin' where?" I questioned in disbelief and my tone had his head snapping up.

"I already see you tryna overthink and shit, but this is legit. My nigga Rob hooked me up with them GMM niggas, they put me on, and I been gettin' to the money ever since." He boasted clearly proud of himself but not realizing that I didn't share in his enthusiasm. Shaking my head I backed away from him like his stupidity was contagious. GMM was the Get Money Mob and from what I'd heard about them they were ruthless as hell and didn't play about their money. I didn't even know how Rob's bum ass was able to get himself involved with them niggas let alone Twan, but I wanted no parts of that shit.

"Aw hell naw, you gots to go for real. I don't know what you and Rob got goin' on with them niggas but I'm not tryna get mixed up in that shit. I'll stick with my job thank you very much." I was already reaching for the doorknob to let him out, no longer interested in even pressing him for my key back, I'd just change the locks.

With his face balled up he stuffed the money back into his pocket and stormed past me to leave, stopping just outside the door. "Fine Dymani, but don't be tryna jump on the bandwagon once you see how much a nigga really start bringing in!" He huffed looking childish as hell as he stomped away. Little did he know his tantrum did nothing for me, and instead of feeding into his bullshit, I slammed and locked the door behind him. For the second time that night a nigga had blown the fuck out of me and I was in even more need of a blunt.

3

KANE

I half listened as my baby brother went on and on about his weed while I returned a few texts. It had been a week since shorty stole his shit, and he was still complaining about it like he hadn't replaced the exotic ass strain a few times already. Truth be told, we made monthly trips out to Cali to cop the best weed they had to offer, so I still wasn't sure why he was whining about a measly ass ounce.

"Man on my soul when I catch that lil thievin' bitch I'm snatchin' her wig off and sellin' it to the highest bidder!" He griped finally pulling my eyes away from my phone screen.

"Nigga what?"

"You heard me. Her ass stole my weed so I'm stealing them tracks right up off her head!" He repeated with a straight face, sounding just as crazy as he had the first time.

"But yo' ass done got that shit back like ten fold, plus didn't you say you had a knot on you and shorty ain't touch not one bill?" I laughed, tucking my phone into my pocket so I could give this fool my full attention. The question had his face twisting up even more.

"So?"

"Nigga so? She could've did you way dirtier and yo' ass out

12

here cryin' over an ounce of Za. Chuck that shit up as a loss and keep it movin' man the fuck?"

"Hell naw! It's the principle behind that shit! Her bald head ass should've never went in my pockets in the first place!" He fumed childishly making me laugh even harder. My indifference to the situation had him grumbling a "fuck you" as he walked off and joined the dice game a couple of our niggas were playing nearby. He'd always been hotheaded, and once he felt like he was wronged, there wasn't shit anybody could tell him. I didn't give a damn about that little weed he was crying about, but I knew he was going to make good on his threat, so all I could do was hope shorty could run as good as she could run a nigga's pockets.

My phone chimed and I quickly pulled it back out to see a text from my realtor that had a wide grin spreading across my face. I'd been in the middle of a bidding war on a commercial property and she'd just informed me that I'd won. The building I was buying I planned to make into a dispensary and it was the perfect location and price. I was out here making big moves and turning everything I touched into a goldmine because the plan was to eventually go legit.

Kendu and I had been running GMM since we jumped off our mama's porch. Our pops had run off on her when she was pregnant with Kendu and although she did everything she could to provide for us it was never enough. We were growing boys so we ate a lot and grew even more. Despite my mama's best efforts there were times we walked out of the house in tight ass clothes and too little shoes. As a teen mom who'd barely made it out of high school she wasn't snagging high paying jobs that would afford us the things we needed. It was actually quite often that we went without, but my mama tried her hardest to make it unnoticeable until she could no longer hide that shit from us. I was fifteen and Kendu was only twelve when we decided to do something about our situation. Being so young we weren't able to get real jobs but I already had my sights set on the drug game. Growing up in Chicago, there was no shortage of niggas hustling on one corner or another, and we wanted what those niggas had. Everything about them shined, their jewelry, their clothes and shoes and definitely the money they flashed. It didn't take much for us to get enticed by the life and before I knew it I'd grown enough courage to holla at the head nigga in charge, Dex. He was responsible for every bit of drugs flowing through the streets and it only made sense to go to him as opposed to anybody that was on a smaller scale. Even at my young age, I knew damn well I wasn't trying to work for another nigga. I wanted all of my profits and the only person I was willing to share them with was my brother. My initiative and hunger was the main reason that Dex said he was willing to take a chance on me and it proved to be one of the smartest decisions he'd ever made.

For five years me and Kendu were his highest earners, bringing in more money than either of us knew what to do with and putting niggas who had been with him for far longer to shame. It didn't take long for his plug, Ricardo to want to meet the young boys that were out selling every other nigga in the city. He felt like it was time for us to move out from under Dex's wings and start our own shit, which was a win-win for everybody..... except Dex didn't see it that way. Although he knew better than to come right out and say it, he didn't want us to become his competition, and so he began waging a silent war against us. We quickly went from that nigga being like a father to us to him being the enemy and once that line was crossed there wasn't no going back. Unfortunately, for him, he underestimated my ability to outsmart him. After getting the green light from Ricardo, I put that nigga to sleep and gained his empire as well as his shipments.

Did I feel bad about what I'd done? Nope. I didn't have an ounce of regret in me and I knew that Kendu didn't either. Killing Dex had been necessary and if it hadn't been him then it would've been us, and I damn sure wasn't ready to go.

The dice game got louder, drawing me out of my thoughts and I couldn't do shit but shake my head at Kendu and our nigga

Quan going back and forth over what his point was. They were both hot headed, and every time they shot dice they got into it, only to turn around and get right back cool. Everybody already knew there wasn't no talking to them niggas when they got like that, so just like me the other four players all stood back laughing as they watched the interaction.

"Man them niggas trippin'!" Our guy Zay huffed shoving what was left of his money into his pocket as he came to a stop at my side.

"Yall already knew they was gone get to arguing, that's why I don't even waste my time shooting with their asses."

"Well this the last time I'm lettin' them talk me into this shit. I ain't even get a chance to win my damn money back." for all the complaining he was doing I knew he'd be right back with the rest of them niggas the next time they pulled out a pair of dice. Before I could call him out on his bullshit though I caught sight of the most gorgeous female I'd ever seen and my words got stuck in my throat. She was bad as hell, even with her doll like features twisted up into an angry ass scowl. Without even knowing her, I wanted to smack the shit out of whoever had put that look on her face. My eyes roamed her body and then landed on the two little hands that were clasped tightly in hers and I scoffed, immediately turned off by the crumb snatchers she had attached to her.

"Oh naw bro, don't even waste yo' time." Zay said realizing that shorty had my eye. "That's Makiyah's lil' fine ass, she a baddie but she a career baby mama too." He tisked as we both eyed her. No lie I was ready to ignore my "no kids rule" for her, but the closer she got the more prominent her belly became proving what he said to be true.

"Damn lil' mama, you shole makin' them babies ain't you?" I grumbled regretfully, and Zay busted out into a fit of laughter that had shorty's face flushing in embarrassment before her previous scowl reappeared.

"Don't worry about my kids.....asshole!" I'm sure she thought she said that last part under her breath, but I heard her loud and clear. Despite the interaction, I found myself still staring after her as she stomped off to the bus stop on the corner. I started to go and snap on the rude ass niggas that remained seated when she got there instead of offering her a seat, but decided against it. *Fuck her smart mouth ass!*

"You a fool for that bro!"

"Man fuck shorty, she better hope I don't beat her baby daddy ass for that smart shit she just said." I frowned finally dragging my eyes away from where she was still standing on the bus stop.

"Shiiit good luck with that, don't nobody know who her baby daddy is, but every time I look up she got a new kid." Zay informed surprising the fuck out of me. I didn't like shorty's mouth, but I still couldn't imagine a nigga keeping her fine ass a secret.

"Damn." Was all I could think to say. I didn't want any kids myself, but if I did ever make some, I definitely wouldn't have them and their mama out here bogus like her baby daddy did. Her situation had fucked up the good mood I'd been in just a few minutes before, and after shaking up with them niggas I told them I'd holla at them later, got in my 2020 Bentley truck, and peeled off. As I passed shorty who was still at the bus stop, I slowed down, contemplating giving her a ride, but the way her face twisted at the sight of my car had me turning up my radio and mashing the gas. I didn't have time for her funky ass attitude, I had more important shit to do like finalizing the paperwork on my building anyway. *Fuck shorty!*

🌿 4 🌿

MAKIYAH

"Cuz, I told you to call me if you needed something. It ain't no reason for you to be out here taking the bus when I got a car!" Dymani chastised as she whipped in and out of traffic. I'd just come from a doctor's appointment that I'd rode two buses and a train to get to with the kids, and she was not happy about it. The fact that my blood pressure was sky high, to the point that Dr. Shapero advised me to get a ride home only added to her irritation.

"I knowwwww but I figured you were asleep after working and-."

"So! You got my whole kid, plus yours and the one you're carrying around riding the bus and the L like I won't drop everything to come get you! Somebody gotta make shit easier on you cause Romell's bum ass sure ain't!" She was on a roll and I didn't even want to interrupt her to let her know that he'd actually broken up with me. That little piece of information would've only had her snapping more, and the last thing I wanted to do was wake up the kids who were silently napping on the backseat. I snuck a glance at them as she continued to rant, glad that they hadn't even so much as stretched in their sleep, before turning my eyes back to the scenery whipping past my window. Dymani didn't know it, but she was making me feel even worse about the position I was in and bringing up Romell was just the icing on the cake. I was out here looking like a damn fool continuously getting pregnant by him and being insulted by random strangers on the street. It hadn't been the first time that someone had assumed that I was just popping out babies back to back, but it definitely hit harder coming from *him*. I'd seen that guy around on a few occasions and each and every time he looked like money. So, for his first time noticing me to be while I was big and pregnant and toting around two more kids and then to speak on it in such a way had me feeling kind of low. I'd never say that I was ashamed of my kids, but I was ashamed of the poor choices that led to me raising them alone without the help of their father.

"Did you hear what I said?" Dymani's voice cut through my thoughts and I turned to see her looking at me expectantly. "Just from that look on your face I can tell you didn't. Where is Romell's trifling ass?" She huffed rolling her eyes and her bringing him up again had me doing the same.

"I don't know Mani, he broke up with me the other day and I ain't seen or heard from him since." I spoke casually like I wasn't beyond hurt by him leaving me and saying some of the things he'd said, but that didn't stop her face from twisting up into a frown.

"What! That raggedy piece of shit! Why didn't you tell me?" She looked like a cartoon character with smoke coming from her ears that's how mad she was. Dymani had never liked Romell and had been telling me from day one that I was too good for him, but you can't tell a bitch that's in love nothing. I let him convince me that she was just jealous because I had a nigga that loved me, some shit straight out of *Baby Boy*. At the time she was going through her own issues with Twan, so it seemed to make sense that she would only have bad things to say about any nigga. Now here I was a few years and one and a half kids later, looking just as stupid as I did back then.

"It's not something I was tryna go around broadcasting bitch. You already don't like him and-."

"And with good reason too! Look at what his lame ass is doin'! Who leaves their baby mama while she's pregnant?"

"I-." I started but she cut me clean off.

"Don't you even think about makin' an excuse for him! You're out here pregnant with high ass blood pressure, and he decides now is the perfect time for him to move on! Tuh! He better hope I don't never see his bitch ass out here! I'm goin' upside his head and I don't give a fuck what you say! Now, are you hungry?" She'd quickly gone from ranting to asking me about food like it wasn't shit and before I could even answer, she was whipping into McDonald's parking lot so sharply, I thought we'd flip over. I was smart enough to know that there wasn't any arguing with her when she got like this, so I remained silent until it was time to order. Truth be told I hadn't been eating the way I should've which probably added to my high blood pressure, but I knew better than to refuse her offer. Already knowing that I'd only take a bite or two of anything I got, I went ahead and ordered a double cheeseburger meal for me and two happy meals for the kids. Dymani happily paid for it all and slipped me a few bills too, forcing me to stuff them in my purse with a stern look.

She was a year younger than me, but no one would be able to tell because she was always acting like the big cousin. Due to having to grow up fast she was very mature for her age, my aunt Yancy, her mama wasn't the best parent and had forced her to take on the role of being the woman of the house before she was even a teenager. Dymani was staying home alone and taking care of her siblings who were just toddlers at the time, while Yancy ran the streets pretending she didn't even have kids. It wasn't long before DCFS got involved though and took them all out of the home, but my Aunt didn't care. I'd gotten lucky enough to have been placed with my grandma on my daddy's side after my parents were both killed in a car accident, which was why I was so sheltered. After losing her only child my granny kept me on a short leash, but since our maternal grandparents had died when we were babies, Dymani and her brothers were split up and put into foster care. Her kids being taken away didn't stop nothing with Yancy though. She was still living her life and turned up pregnant again just a couple of years ago. Not only did she find her now grown daughter, but she ended up leaving Armani with her and she'd been raising her ever since. You couldn't tell Dymani that wasn't her baby and after losing her brothers to the system I didn't blame her at all.

There was plenty of times I wished that I was more like my little cousin. More outspoken and more levelheaded as opposed to being overly emotional and wearing my heart on my sleeve. I knew at the moment though that my pregnancy played a big role in my current emotional state, and I couldn't wait until it was over.

By the time Dymani finally pulled up to my apartment to drop us off I had made it up in my mind that I was going to do a better job of being more like her, but the sight of a silver Ford Focus parked in front of my door caught my attention.

"Oh I know the fuck he didn't!" Dymani had peeped the same thing as me and was already on go mode.

"Nah, he's probably just drove hisself over here to get the rest of his stuff cuz." I quickly tried to explain, but she wasn't trying to hear that. She gave me the side eye and hopped out just as Romell emerged from the front door with none other than Simone walking behind him carrying a box. As soon as they saw us they paused in their steps, but Dymani was already rounding the car with her fists balled up. I barely had time to take off my seat belt before she'd swung and a full blown fight ensued. By the time I struggled out of the car and made it over to them, Dymani had Simone on the ground as she sat on top of her giving her all face shots.

"Get yo' ass off my bitch!" Romell finally snapped out of his trance and yanked her away, damn near flinging her small frame across the yard.

"Oh hell nah!" I screeched jumping onto his back as he bent down to help a bloody Simone. Just the fact that he was taking such extra care with her, when just the other day he was fighting me like I wasn't carrying his child had me heated, and I tried to take that shit out on his face. Since I couldn't swing and hold onto him at the same time I dug into his exposed skin hoping to draw blood. As he slung me around trying to get me off, Dymani gained her composure and came over throwing punches.

I guess Romell got tired of getting his ass beat though because he finally wrestled my arms from around his neck making me land hard on the grass and I immediately felt a sharp pain shoot across my abdomen.

"Ahhhhhh!"

My screams seemed to make everyone stand still and Dymani's eyes damn near popped out of her head at the sight of blood filling the light blue biker shorts I was wearing. "Look at what the fuck you did!" She shouted at a stunned Romell who still hadn't moved as she rushed to my side. Without any confirmation I already knew I was losing my baby. The amount of blood and severe cramping told me that there wouldn't be anything that could be done, even as Dymani frantically called 911 and Romell shoved Simone in the car and sped off. I'd just said that I was going to do better and just that fast my plans had been thrown out of the window.

5

ROMELL

I kept looking in the rear view as I drove off, only partially considering turning around while Simone whimpered beside me assessing her wounds. It wasn't that I didn't care about my baby, but from what I could see it was already too late to do anything about it anyway. If there was a reason to go back it would've been to choke the shit out of Makiyah for jumping her dumb ass into a fight while she was pregnant in the first place. She'd definitely been acting out in ways she never would've before and I knew it had everything to do with her thot ass cousin.

Six months ago a muthafucka couldn't pay me to believe that Makiyah would fight me, let alone call me out on my bullshit but that's all she'd been doing lately. Hell, her normally docile manner was partly to blame for me starting to fuck around with Simone. At first, that sweet naïve shit had been a straight turn on after dealing with bitches with a lot of attitude and big mouths. I liked that she did what I told her and believed everything I said, but shit started going downhill when she had our son. She got lazy as hell and started expecting me to do more than she was doing. It seemed like she always had an excuse as to why she couldn't take her ass to work and then once she got pregnant this time around with our daughter, shit really got bad. She always complained about being tired and between the dirty house and lack of food I didn't know what irritated me more!

A certain sense of obligation had kept me around this long, but truthfully, I'd outgrown Makiyah a year ago. I had a bitch that actually liked to work, kept herself and her crib up and gave me peace whenever I was around. I wouldn't go so far as to say that I regretted RJ, but I damn sure regretted who I'd picked to be his mama and if our daughter did die, she'd probably be better off. Makiyah didn't deserve to carry anymore of my kids and she damn sure didn't have no business raising a female.

"We need to go to the hospital Ro!" Simone cried out and I took my eyes off the road long enough to give her a once over. Even though Dymani had just went to work on her face, her beauty was undeniable. My ass felt lucky as hell to have bagged a bitch like her, just doing something as simple as stopping through the corner store for some blunts. As soon as I laid eyes on her smooth caramel skin and thick ass body in her pink skirt suit, I knew I had to have her. She looked high class as fuck, and after finding out that she worked at a bank, I understood why. Shorty was young and getting it and much more deserving of my seed which was why I was shooting up her club every chance I got resulting in her being two months pregnant.

"What's wrong you crampin' or something?"

"No, but I wanna check on my baby after you let that silly ass bitch just attack me!" It was clear she had an attitude, and I understood why but I didn't want her stressing and shit. I'd already lost one baby that day I wasn't trying to lose another.

"You know I ain't *let* a muhfucka do shit! Fuck you wanted me to do, I already just made Makiyah probably lose the baby-."

"So you care more about her dirty ass than me?" She shrieked pointing her perfectly manicured finger at herself and I blew out a frustrated breath.

"You know damn well that ain't the case, if it was I wouldn't be in this fuckin' car with yo' ass right now."

"Yeah but-."

"But nothin! If you not feelin' like something is wrong then it ain't no point in goin' to the hospital! I could be bouta go to jail for that shit back there and you want me to run right into them muhfuckas in the emergency room! You want me to go to jail or some shit?" I questioned looking back and forth between her and the street. Of course, I knew that me getting locked up was the last thing she wanted, but I was desperate as hell. Makiyah would never tell the boys on me, but if Dymani was with her she'd damn sure run her mouth and my black ass would be in cuffs before the night was out. My best shot was to try and convince Simone not to go, at least until I talked to Makiyah first.

Immediately she looked regretful and I had to stop myself from grinning proudly as she tried to reassure *me*. "Of course, I don't want you getting arrested! We have a baby on the way Ro!" She said blinking back tears and just to add a little bit more sauce I lifted her hand into mine and kissed it.

"Okay well, then let's go home until we figure out what's what, and if you start feeling like something is wrong, then we'll go later." I softened up my tone laying it on extra thick and just like I knew she would, she went along with it, bobbing her head up and down in agreement. This was why she was winning the race to a nigga's heart over Makiyah. Simone was everything I thought my baby mama would be smart, ambitious and most of all, she allowed me to lead. Little did she know I'd already been driving towards her crib anyway. I had shit to do and that whole scene with Makiyah had set me back a little as far as time.

Suddenly my phone was going off in my pocket and I could feel Simone's eyes on me just waiting for me and try to answer, thinking it was my other baby mama. I already knew it wasn't nobody but Noah's ass trying figure out where I was. I'd told him I'd be finished moving the rest of my shit by one and I'd call him, but it was now past two. His ass had been stressing since the night before when we'd ran up in one of the GMM traps. Me on the other hand, I wasn't worried at all. Unbeknownst to him, I'd been planning on robbing them niggas since I ran into Twan's stupid ass and he got to running off at the mouth about how much he was making at the trap he worked in. It had only taken a few key questions to get all the information I needed to put a plan in motion. The plan had been to do the shit myself, so that I could reap all the awards, but I quickly realized I'd need some type of help from someone I could trust. As scary as Noah was, he was also the most loyal nigga I knew and it was only right that I took him along. I went in straight blasting, killing everything moving in that bitch and once I had all three of the niggas in there laid down except one, he calmed down a bit. I even let him do the honors of killing the last one after he told us where to find the money and drugs, but really I'd done it so that his scary ass wouldn't be inclined to rat me out without knowing that he was going down too.

We walked away with three keys and a good sixty grand, and I hadn't even been expecting all that. According to Twan, they made good money there, but it was only about twenty racks a week. Regardless, it had been my lucky day going in there when I did, but now that we had that shit, we needed to figure out our next move. Which was why Noah was hitting me up at the moment.

"Stop lookin' at me like that, it's just Noah." I grunted pulling my phone out and showing her the screen. Just like I'd said Noah was the one calling but she still raised a questioning brow.

"Why aren't you answering then?" she wanted to know. The suspicious look she was giving me had my nose turned up aggravated. Normally, Simone was extremely secure, even when I was still living with Makiyah. I didn't know if it was the pregnancy or what but I didn't like her lack of confidence and I started not to even answer her but decided to reassure her anyway.

"I'm not answering cause I already know what his ass want. We was 'sposed to meet up, but that shit back at the house got me runnin' late." I blew out a frustrated breath as I pulled into her designated parking spot and pushed the gear into park. "You don't have to keep questioning me. I'm here with yo' ass bae, you won. Now come bring yo' sexy ass in this house." Compliments were the quickest way to get her past whatever issues we were having and this time was no different. She tried to hide her smile, but I caught it returning one to her before helping her out the car.

After getting that out of the way, I helped her inside and into bed with the instructions for her to rest. I already knew that she wasn't going to be happy about me leaving, so I mixed some melatonin in with a cup of juice I brought her. It didn't take any time for her ass to be snoring beside me and I was free.

The first stop I made once I left was to my mama's to check on the money and shit I had stashed there, and then it was off to see Noah. I was barely able to park good before he was snatching the door open and coming out to meet me on the porch. Just from the look in his eyes, I knew some shit had happened.

"Man what the fuck-?"

"Nigga, I been blowin' you the fuck up! Where yo' ass been!" he seethed, lighting up a cigarette and pacing the porch.

"I got caught up with my baby mamas and Dymani, nothin' major, but I'm here now. What's up?" he shook his head, not bothering to say anything as he continued to smoke.

"I heard them niggas Kane and Kendu out for blood! They already done went and put out a bounty for us for twenty bands each." His fingers shook as he spoke.

"For *us*, or for whoever hit 'em?" I needed clarification. There wasn't a bitch made bone in my body, however it would be smart for me to be two steps ahead of them niggas. Shit the way Noah was acting, I wasn't even sure how far his loyalty would stretch and I damn sure wasn't trying to be in a war all by myself.

"For whoever brings them the heads of the niggas that was dumb enough to rob 'em muhfucka!" Despite not being afraid, I couldn't help but breathe a sigh of relief. Knowing that the GMM wasn't yet aware of who we were gave me a little more time, but not much and clearly Noah was ready to crack if some-body applied even the slightest amount of pressure. Looking at him, I realized I'd probably end up being the one to kill his ass, because at the moment he was the weakest link. It'd definitely be a shame for a nigga to die just because he was scary, but fuck it, it was either going to be him or me, and I wasn't dying because of loose lips. I played it cool though and threw on a reassuring grin.

"Niiiigggga, you trippin'. Even if they do got a hit out, don't nobody know about this shit but me and you. As long as you keep yo' mouth shut and don't be spendin' unnecessary money we gon' be straight." I shrugged and he looked at me doubtfully.

"Man bro, you sure?"

"Come on now, I wouldn't have done the shit if I thought it was any chance we'd get caught bro, we good. We just gon' lay low for a couple days then head out to Miami where yo' cousins at." The mention of leaving and going to by his peoples had him visibly less stressed,- and I hoped them niggas wasn't as scary as his ass or else I'd have even more problems.

"You right." He nodded letting my words sink in and for the second time that day I had to mentally pat myself on the back at how good I was at spitting game.

"I know I am. Just stick to the plan and we gon' be straight." I'd once again put out another fire and just to put him more at ease I stuck around for a little bit longer just shooting the breeze before shaking up with him and moving on to my next destina-tion. Hopefully, shit went just as smooth with Makiyah as it did with everyone else.

🐦 6 🐦

KENDU

I paced the floor behind my brother as he questioned the niggas Twan and Rob, gripping my gun tightly. Kane was expecting some type of confession, but I didn't need one for what I was about to do to their asses. In my mind they were guilty by association, whether they had something to do with it or not, the simple fact that neither of them were working the day the trap got hit made them suspect as hell. But you couldn't tell my brother that. Kane thought he was Obama, always trying to talk through some shit when I was more of the shoot first ask questions never type. At the moment, I wanted nothing more than to decorate the walls and floor with their brain matter, but my brother didn't believe they had shit to do with the botched ass robbery. His logic was that they weren't dumb enough to rob the trap on their day off because off top it would make them look guilty. He was on some *Criminal Minds* type shit, trying to do case studies and I was over it. We'd already been in the musty ass basement we were holding them in for over two hours. Our whole team had taken turns beating their heads in and they still hadn't said shit that could've been considered helpful, but again, that wasn't stopping Kane.

"Man fuck this, just get it over with bro! These niggas ain't bouta tell you shit!" I fumed stopping my movement long enough to shoot an evil glare their way.

"I got this Du' fall back." his calm tone did nothing but piss me off more. I'd never try to undermine my brother in front of our workers, but he was acting like we weren't out over a hundred grand! True enough we wiped our asses with that type of money, but he knew how I got down and no matter how small the portion was, taking from me was something I didn't tolerate! I wasn't trying to hear shit but these niggas take their last breath and he was wasting all of our time.

"Yeah, ayite." I said loud enough for only his muscle head ass to hear. Instead of responding he shot me a warning look and focused his attention back on our victims.

"Y'all see this nigga ready to slump y'all asses and it's only so long I can hold him back. Now we can make this shit quick and easy or I can burn y'all alive, ain't neither gon make a difference to me, just tell us what you know."

"Man, I got a girl and a baby man, please don't do this shit! I swear I don't know shit about no robbery! I wouldn't do no goofy shit like that!" Twan was crying real tears as he pleaded for his life and that nor the mention of his family moved me in the slightest. I was still going to murk his ass and probably fuck his bitch if I could find her.

"Fuck that, this nigga been running his mouth to anybody that'll listen about how he gettin' money! Ain't no tellin' who the fuck ran up in y'all shit cause of him, his ass just as guilty as whoever did it, but y'all know I been down since day one! Everything was cool til' I brought this nigga in the mix-!"

"AhhhhhhAhhhh!"

As soon as Rob was done with his little speech I sent a bullet through the side of his head, instantly making his body crumple to the floor and Twan started screaming like a bitch and throwing up all over his self. That nigga had sealed his own fate with me by throwing his mans under the bus. He'd said all of that and still hadn't said much, but just the way he'd gone about it had taken my already fucked up mood to it's boiling point. "Shut yo' cryin' ass up! That nigga just sold you the fuck out and you up in here screamin' and cryin' like a bitch!" I sneered looking at him in disgust. He was smart enough to cut out all the wailing and shit, but his ass was still sniveling and begging for us not to kill him. The way he was acting I was sure that what Rob said was true and his pussy ass was out there telling people our business. Just like I'd done his "boy" I gave him one to the dome without a warning as well, silencing him forever.

"Man somebody clean this shit up, and the rest of y'all niggas can go, but keep y'all ear to the streets and make sure niggas know the bounty doubled!" Kane barked waving them out dismissively. As if that shit was rehearsed or something, four of our low-level workers immediately went over and began lifting the bodies while everyone else filed out. "Nigga what the fuck, I said to fall back!" Kane had waited until the room was cleared before stepping in my face with a look that could kill.

"Man, I ain't tryna hear that shit, you know just like I do them niggas had to go-."

"Yeah but what the fuck I say! Yo' hotheaded ass gotta chill, cause now we back at square fuckin' one, with no money, no drugs and nobody to hold accountable!" he was mad as hell, spitting and shit and all I was thinking about was finally getting the fuck up out of there. As soon as I'd put the bullets in their heads those niggas were forgotten and it was on to the next.

"I ain't gotta do shit! We out money and product, so somebody gotta pay and today it was them niggas, tomorrow its gon' be somebody else until we find our shit. You already know a muhfucka ain't gon' be able to sit on that shit for too long and me and my bitch gon' be ready whenever they ass come out of hiding!" I told him lifting my gun.

"Nah, we ain't killin' nobody else unless we sure that it's the right person."

"But-."

"But nothin nigga. A killin' spree ain't good for business right now and we still gotta get off this last load. I gotta go drop this money off and you need to clean this shit up." he motioned to the two puddles of blood on the floor before walking off and leaving me alone in the basement. As soon as the door closed behind his ass,I pulled out my phone and called up the cleaning crew. I wished the fuck I would scrub up them bum nigga's blood. I didn't even wait for them to arrive, I just got the fuck up outta there.

This shit had me over blown and I needed a blunt and some wet pussy to slide up in. By the time I made it to my matte black, Range Rover, I already had my favorite little freak on the phone. "Aye, you home?" I asked as soon as she picked up. I didn't have time for small talk and she already knew what time it was.

"Yeah, I just got in from-."

"Ayite, hop in the shower, I'm on my way." Without waiting for a response, I hung up and drove off towards her crib in Bucktown. I stopped on the way and grabbed a few empties so I could roll up once I got there and not even a half hour later I was circling her block looking for a parking spot. It had been a minute since I'd been over there and I was beginning to see why when after the third time around I still hadn't seen anywhere to pull into that was close to her building. Just when I was about to say 'fuck it' and call somebody else to slide on, I spotted a woman struggling to get two little kids in her car. My first instinct as I pulled up was to curse her the fuck out for having them kids outside this late, but I wasn't in the mood to be going back and forth with a bitch about another nigga kids. Instead, I sat waiting for her to finally get them in their seats growing increasingly more irritated with how long that shit was taking.

"Aye, hurry the fuck up, I got shit to do!" I hit the horn and yelled out the window. She instantly stood straight up, giving me a perfect view of her face as she squinted my way. I hadn't been expecting for her to be fine as fuck though and even her mean mug was sexy as hell.

"Nigga fuck you!" she hollered back, raising her middle finger up and now I was the one squinting. For some reason shorty looked familiar as hell, but I couldn't place where I knew her from and before I could think too much on it, she was in her car and pulling away. Shaking the encounter off, I took her spot and double-checked for my gun and blunts.

Ashlee was already standing at the door waiting for me when I finally made it up her steps, and I took a moment to check her out. She was dressed in a lacy black bra and panty set with the Savage Fenty emblem hanging from them both and some clear stripper heels. As usual, her hair was perfectly curled and hanging down her back, as she tossed it over her shoulder and smirked sexily.

"Hey daddy." She purred, pulling me inside.

"What's good baby?" I'd already forgotten about the shit that had just gone down as I dropped a quick kiss on her neck, making her giggle. Besides looking good and keeping herself together, I liked fucking with Ashlee because she was a clean ass woman with her own everything. It was a bonus that she didn't have any kids or baby daddies lurking around, which meant that she could give me all of her attention. She led me through the small living room, and I plopped down on the couch so I could roll up and smoke before I tore her pussy up.

"Let me roll for you baby, and you just relax." she said reaching for the blunt and ounce of weed I'd pull out, but I quickly held it away from her reach.

"Nah I got it. Last time I let a bitch near my Za, she stole it." My words trailed off as I realized that the bitch outside had been the same one who'd stolen my weed! It had been a while since that night, and a bunch of other shit had popped up that had put that situation to the back of my mind, so it hadn't registered right away. I cursed under my breath, pissed that I'd been so close to shorty and had let her bald-headed ass slip through my fingers.

"When was you with a bitch Du?" Ashlee questioned,

frowning already getting in nag mode and reminding me of the one thing I didn't like about her ass. Despite me telling and showing her that we were just fuck buddies, she thought she had rights to me and my dick. She was jealous as hell and didn't hesitate to ask me about other bitches, case in point.

"You worried 'bout the wrong shit bro. I came over here to get some pussy. You tryna fuck, or you tryna argue, cause I can call somebody else that got better parking and knows their role?" knowing I was serious, she sat back on the couch and folded her arms, pouting.

"Fine!" she huffed.

"I hope yo' attitude better when I come back too." I tossed over my shoulder, heading to the bathroom down the hall. Obviously, she needed a minute to get herself together, and my ass needed to go get shorty off my mind. It was crazy that I was more upset that I hadn't caught up with her fine ass than I even was about the weed anymore, and that definitely wasn't like me. As soon as I got inside of the bathroom, I wiped a hand down my face and released a sigh, but some shit sitting on the sink had me turned right back up. I picked up the little white stick, knowing what it was, yet still hoping I was wrong. "Yo' Ash, what the fuck is this!" I barked, stomping back into the living room where she was sitting with a shocked look on her face.

"I'm pregnant," she shrugged uncomfortably. "And it's definitely yours."

A nigga whole night had just gone from bad to worse and I was instantly regretting even calling her ass up at this point.

❧ 7 ❧

DYMANI
FOUR WEEKS LATER...

I was playing Ann Marie loud as hell on my way to Makiyah's house, because that was my mind frame. Twan had brought his ass over talking all that shit, and I hadn't heard from him once since then! He was the main reason why I didn't believe shit nigga's said now because they were always lying. Now I just needed my cousin to be on the same type of time as me because it was obvious Romell wasn't coming back.

After him and that pathetic bitch Simone made her miscarry, she stayed in the hospital and had to deliver a dead baby, only for him to turn around and try to keep her quiet about it. She was much better than me because he would've been under the jail. Shit, I might have added a little bit more sauce to it too. Makiyah, on the other hand, granted his request like a fool and had now spent the last month in a tragic ass depressed state. It was so bad that I had to take Rj to my house with Armani and me because she couldn't even take care of him in her condition. However, today she was getting up and getting back to life, even if I had to drag her ass out of the bed myself.

She didn't know it, but after having to call out so much, since I didn't have nobody to get the kids, I was in need of a job. Although I did have a little cushion to hold me over, it wasn't nearly enough, and I had been actively looking for another club to do bottle service at. Hell, I was even willing to shake some ass if I needed to because the bag needed to be secured! I'd been lucky to get my neighbor Ms. Celine to watch the kids for a while so that I could go to an interview at club Eclipse and I was praying I got it.

I pulled up in front of Makiyah's and hurried inside past the bum ass niggas that were standing out front. Even in some distressed jeans and a simple crop top I had them calling out for my number, but after Twan a nigga was the last thing on my mind. Since I had a key, I was able to walk right in, and my nose instantly turned up from the smell of garbage. I'd been over just a couple of days before and hadn't noticed the odor, but obviously Makiyah had really let shit go. I stepped over the same toys that the kids had played with last time we were there and made my way to her bedroom where the door was shut tight.

"Nah, get yo' ass up Ky!" I fussed busting inside to find her buried under a mountain of blankets. It was a pigsty in there, with plates of food, trash, and piles of clothes everywhere. If I wasn't so pissed I'd have been ready to shed some tears at how far back this nigga had set my cousin. No doubt she was battling depression before, but it seemed to have gotten worse since she lost the baby and seemingly Romell in the same day. Looking around it was clear that her ass needed an intervention, and I was just the bitch to give it to her.

"Gon' Dymani I'm sleep!" her voice sounded from under the covers, and I wasted no time snatching them away.

"Hell nah! You in here bouta die and that nigga out there livin' his best life! Yo' ass ain't called me to even check up on RJ, and you know that's some bullshit! I know you're hurting, shit, I'm hurting for you, but you gotta keep going! My lil' cousin is depending on you cause he damn sure can't depend on his daddy and you in here hiding from the world! Fuck Romell! That nigga ain't been here anyway, you ain't losing shit but a leech with him gone for real, and as far as the baby, God don't make no mistakes. You might not want to see it that way, but I'm gone always keep it real with you. Life was hard enough on you with just Rj, it would've been that much harder with two babies, plus you don't need another tether to that no good ass nigga!" the mention of the baby had tears pooling in her eyes, but like I said I was going to keep it all the way funky with her.

"That was my baby too tho Mani! I was going to get out and do what I needed to for both my kids without Romell! This ain't got shit to do with him!"

"And I get that but look around boo. You bout ain't been out the bed since you been home besides to get food and shit." I told her, motioning to her messy surroundings. "I know you hurt about losing the baby, but Rj is still here, and he needs you. Even when we came the other day, you barely lifted your head to acknowledge him. He's probably just as hurt as you because he been ain't had his daddy, and now he's losing the only constant in his life." I could tell that my words were sinking in as her face fell, and she cried harder.

"It just hurts soooooo baaaaad!" she wailed, covering her face with her hands. I wrapped my arms around her shuddering shoulders and pulled her into a tight embrace while she let out all of her frustrations.

"I know, but you have to keep going. You have to get up every day and try to do better for you and yo' baby even when it hurts. You're the only one that provides for him, so you have to go hard; he deserves that."

"I don't even know where to start." Her cries had now turned to sniffles as she looked around, probably just now realizing how much of a mess she'd made.

"Wellll, you can start in the shower 'cause you a lil' tart boo, and then we'll go from there." I chuckled honestly, and her eyes widened before she laughed a little herself.

"Uh yeah, let me go handle that." I nodded in agreement as she climbed off the bed headed for the bathroom.

"You might wanna do a bath and add some bleach to the

water too hoe!" I called out after her, and she flipped me the finger.

"Fuck you bitch!"

She seemed like she was in a better mood, but I knew that with depression that shit went up and down. I was glad that I was able to at least get her out of bed and feeling positive about the future. I'd been on my paperchase so hard that I hadn't really been a good cousin lately, but I was going to make sure I was there for her going forward.

While she handled her hygiene, I started to pick up the mess around her room. I knew that clutter always made the situation worse, and I wanted her to stay upbeat. It really took no time at all for her room to look and smell better, and by the time she stepped out of the shower, I didn't even recognize it. "You didn't have to clean up for me Dymani, I could've-."

"Yeah, but I wanted to and if we're gonna make it to this interview, then we don't got no time to waste." I shrugged, checking the time on my watch. Even though I'd made it so that I had time to fight with her if I needed to, we were still short on time and had only about an hour to get to the club.

"What you mean 'we' bitch?" her brows dipped, and she stopped rifling through her drawers long enough to look my way.

"I mean what I said hoe, I got an interview, but it won't hurt for you to come along and see if they have any other open positions," I mentioned casually, hoping that she didn't feel so caught off guard that she'd clam up and not want to go. "Now hurry up before you make me late." She narrowed her eyes but did as I said and finished getting dressed. After she slipped into the black jeans and t-shirt, I nodded my approval already loving how much better she looked.

A month later and all of the little baby weight she'd gained had fallen off, and she was back to her original size nine. I just knew that with her body, if they didn't have a position for her they'd fuck around and make one up. A little bit of gel on her baby hairs and the jumbo box braids that I'd done the day she came home from the hospital were looking brand new. You wouldn't have been able to tell that this was the same woman I'd come in and found balled up in the fetal position just a half-hour before. My bitch looked good no makeup, no lashes just all-natural.

The same niggas that had been catcalling me when I'd gotten there were damn near drooling when we walked out to my car. Makiyah ignored them just like I had, probably not even realizing how damn fine she was. We made it to the club in no time, and I damn near had to drag her in. Her nerves were starting to show, but we'd made it this far, and I wasn't going to let her turn around at this point.

The inside of the club was just as lavish and upscale as I remembered, and I was getting excited just thinking about how it'd look at night all lit up. It was just the type of place that ballers would frequent and pay top dollar.

"Can I help y'all?" who I assumed was a bartender asked from behind the bar, never stopping the wiping she was doing. I instantly detected the attitude in her tone and knew that if I got the job she'd be one of them hating bitches that everybody worked with.

"Yeah, I have an interview with Sean. Can you let him know Dymani is here?" I didn't miss the way she rolled her eyes before turning around to make the call to her boss, and I shared a look with Makiyah. Either she and Sean had some freaky shit going on, or she felt threatened by our presence, and if it was the latter, I definitely couldn't blame her dusty ass. I kept a phony smirk on my face as I waited for Sean to make his presence known.

"He said come on up." She pointed towards the stairs and continued cleaning up without giving us any more of her attention. It was a good thing that besides his office, there was only one other room up there, and his name was on the door. I knocked twice before entering to find him sitting behind his desk, and as soon as he laid eyes on both Makiyah and me, he lit up. Me on the other hand, I was extremely disappointed. He'd sounded sexy as hell over the phone, but in person, he looked like a bigger version of Murda Pain, and not even the jewels or expensive clothes did anything to make him look better.

"Hey, welcome ladies, I didn't know I was getting two for the price of one!" He grinned and rubbed his hands together.

"No, but you can get two for the price of two." I quipped using a sugary tone. "My cousin, Makiyah, came along just in case you have something else available." His lustful stare bounced between the two of us before settling on her, and I could just about imagine what he was thinking.

"I might be able to find something for her. You know how to dance-?"

"Nah I was thinking more along the lines of bottle service or even a bartender." I quickly shut him down and he sighed dejectedly.

"You're in luck, I did lose a bartender this week. You got any experience?"

"Uhhh no, but I'm a quick learner and-."

"Good, Y'all can start tonight. Be here at ten." He said, dropping two employee packets on his desk and dismissing us with a wave of his hand. Just like that a bitch was back on!

⚘ 8 ⚘

MAKIYAH

It had been a week since I started working at the club, and I
had to admit that keeping busy made it easier to push
thoughts of Romell and our baby to the back of my mind.
When I wasn't working, I was sleeping or spending time with Rj,
but there had been moments when I hadn't been able to run
from the pain. It would creep up on me, and I'd allow myself to
feel every bit of it, but it was no longer swallowing me whole.

Dymani had really saved me when she came in that day and
forced me out of bed. All this time, I'd been keeping her at arm's
length because of how much I loved Romell. Despite everything
he'd done and said, I didn't want her to know just how bad
things were. That didn't matter though, because there was just
some things I couldn't hide or explain away, and she always saw
right through that shit. Maybe she was just able to see Romell
for his works, while I was still wearing rose-colored glasses when
it came to him. Or maybe it had always been there, and I'd
ignored every sign that God had tried to send my way. Whatever
it was, I appreciated her caring enough to pull me out of my
funk, even if it was against my will.

Since we were both at the club during the same hours, we'd
worked something out with Ms. Celine to keep the kids for us.

After the first time she'd babysat, she'd fallen in love with them though so it didn't take much to convince her.

"Hey, I'm gon' need you to handle this end of the bar while I go to the bathroom." The other bartender, Kya shouted in my ear and switched off before I could agree. She'd been nasty to us ever since the first day we'd walked in, and the rumors around the club confirmed our suspicions that it was because she had something going on with Sean. I usually paid her rudeness little to no attention, but I definitely planned to give her ugly ass a piece of my mind when she returned. Blowing out a frustrated breath, I finished the order that I was already making and then worked my way down to her end.

Twenty minutes later, I still hadn't caught myself up and was just about ready to walk off to go find her ass when she came limping back with a dreamy look on her face. I instantly turned my nose up, knowing that she'd just snuck off for a quickie with Sean's fat ass. Rolling my eyes, I moved back down to my end, hoping that she'd at least washed her nasty ass hands before coming back to work.

"Hey boo, how you doin?" Dymani squeezed behind the bar and asked as I continued handing off drinks. As soon as I'd finished, another wave of clubgoers approached waving their money in the air, and I sucked my teeth in irritation.

"Fuckin' blue Sean's cheap ass knows this is too much bar for just me and that bitch, especially when she's always creepin' her nasty tail upstairs to sit on that nigga's dick." I spat, not even caring if any of the customers heard me. Dymani frowned just like I had a few minutes before and looked down towards the end that Kya was at.

"Ugh, he gotta be breaking her off some serious coint for her to be willin' to sit on that ole' funky ass dick." She shook her head, and I couldn't help but laugh at the look of disgust on her face.

"Bitch you a fool!"

"Shiiiit, I'm serious! Who the hell would fuck Sean for free?

Tuh! That bitch a fool, and any other bitch in here that's sittin' on that lil' Vienna sausage!" I was laughing so hard that I wasn't even measuring my drinks right.

"I'm not bouta play with yo' ass tonight Dymani. Don't you got some bottles to serve or somethin'?"

"Oh, that's why I came down here. The nigga's that got booth five got a big ass order, and they gon' be here in like fifteen minutes." She spoke nonchalantly, popping her gum between each word. Her ass always came trying to get me to help with her orders instead of getting one of the other bottle girls like she was supposed to. At first, I thought it was because she wanted to keep an eye on me during work since we only ever saw each other in passing, but I quickly learned that wasn't the case. She was really coming to get me to ensure I got the tips over everyone else, with her sneaky ass.

"You see this line? Ain't no way I'm gon' be able to leave, especially with Kya working the other end."

"Girl fuck her! She left you down here while she went and hopped on that lil' Vienna sausage! She can handle this shit by herself for a few!" she huffed, glaring the girl's way again.

"How you know it's lil bitch, let me find out you done seen what Sean got to offer!" Her face balled up until it was almost unrecognizable, and I laughed harder.

"Don't play with me like that! I almost just threw the fuck up!" She gagged. "I won't never be that desperate!"

"Aye you never know, the way he got Kya's ass acting he might put it down." I continued to fuck with her as I filled up five shot glasses for the guy in front of me, and she began gathering the order for the VIP.

"I'm gone crack yo' ass with this Hennessy, you keep it up!" She threatened holding up the bottle for emphasis, and I quickly held my hands in surrender.

"Okay, okay, Ima leave you alone!" Laughing, I finished up another order. It felt good to laugh, and with Dymani keeping me company, it seemed like I was able to clear my end of the bar quicker.

Before I knew it, almost twenty minutes had passed, and the special guests she had been waiting on were due to arrive any minute. "Aye Kya, Ky's bouta help me with this order! She'll be right back!" She yelled down to the other end, gaining a nasty look from Kya, who had suddenly become swamped.

"Oh hell naw! It's too busy, and she ain't sposed to be helping you anyway!"

"Girl, just cause you fuckin' the owner don't mean you got some authority around here, she sposed to work, and that's what she doin'!" Before Kya could think of something to say back, Dymani had already handed me one of the fully loaded trays and motioned for me to go. I didn't need to look back to know that she was right behind me as I made my way through the crowd. As usual niggas we're pulling at me and trying to cop feels, despite knowing I was working. At first, I was flattered by the attention. It was definitely something I hadn't gotten in a very long time, but after dealing with handsy, drunk niggas every night I quickly got tired of that shit.

I managed to dodge their advances and make it to the section without spilling a single item from the heavy ass tray and as just as we finished setting it all up when the music came to an abrupt stop.

"Awwwww shit! Them GMM niggas in the building! Y'all niggas better cuff yo' girls cause they lookin' like money!" the Dj came over the mic before cutting on *Bank* by Lil Baby, and I looked at Dymani with an eye roll. We'd had plenty of ballers step through the doors since I'd started, but none of them had gotten the same reception as these niggas, and I was instantly turned off by the bravado. I had no clue who they were or what made them so special that they got theme music when they entered, but I was hoping they paid like they apparently weighed because I had full intentions on taking Rj somewhere special the next day. We both deserved some carefree fun, and I was going to make sure we got it.

From where we were, we couldn't really make out the men of the hour, since the crowd around them was so thick, but anticipating that they'd be up in less than a minute, we lit our bottles and started dancing as we held them up. Taking a cue from Dymani I started throwing my ass in a circle, and it wasn't long before the area was filled with a bunch of niggas. They were already tossing us bills and shit like we were strippers, and I was getting geeked just seeing the cash piling up. There wasn't any shame in me as I set the bottles down and began picking up my money so that I could go back down to the bar since I was sure that Kya was already fuming.

"Bitch you got me fucked up!"

I'd been so distracted, adding up my cut, that I hadn't been aware of the altercation happening behind me until I heard Dymani shouting and the reaction of the crowd. I looked up to find my cousin, wigless with her rough braids showing as she was held back by one of the niggas in the section. She was going back and forth with a fine ass nigga who just so happened to be holding her wig as he got restrained too. It took me a second to wrap my mind around the scene before me, but once I finally snapped out of it and ran over to try to help.

"Dymani what the hell? Are you okay?"

"Her thievin' ass fine, but she better run me my Za, or she gon' be finishin' her shift with them Cleo braids!" the guy said, shaking her wig in front of her teasingly.

"Boy fuck you! That weed was the least you could give a bitch after yo' limp dick ass fell asleep on me! Ole' noodle dick ass nigga!" Dymani sent the entire section into a fit of laughter, only pissing him off more, and he fought to get out of his restraints.

"Bitch you a baldheaded lie! This muhfucka stay hard!" he shouted, grabbing his crotch since it was obvious that the guy holding him wasn't going to let him past. It was then that I realized the nigga holding him back was none other than the one I'd cursed out on the block a while back. Instantly my mood soured upon recognizing him. It was no wonder them two disrespectful ass niggas hung out. They both were rude and did whatever they wanted to.

"Ha! Probably only when you pop a Viagra nigga! Yo' ass must've forgotten to take yo' medicine before we got to the hotel!"

"Oooookay, let's go before we fuck around and get fired," I told her completely over their arguing at this point. They were doing the most, and I knew that eventually Sean would be wobbling his ass over soon. I grabbed her arm, ready to drag her out of there if I needed to, and the guy that was holding her quickly let her go.

"Bitch I ain't goin' nowhere til' I get my damn wig back!" she snatched away and stood with her arms folded, making me roll my eyes before turning and asking.

"Can she please have her wig back?" I sighed at just how ridiculous the question was, but there was no other less embarrassing way to ask. The two men had a private conversation, and I could tell that *my asshole* was trying to convince *Dymani's asshole* to give her, her shit back. Whatever he said had him handing over the wig reluctantly, and as I passed it along to my cousin, who threw it right back on. He seemed to suddenly realize who I was. His eyes narrowed in recognition.

"Don't I know you?" he questioned, stepping into my personal space, and I instantly backed up.

"Uhh no. Let's go Dymani." My voice shook a little as I lied. Somehow even though I couldn't stand him, the lustful way he looked at my body had me nervous and my heart pounding.

"Ohhh yeah. You shorty with all the kids!" he paused stopping me from walking off by grabbing my hand and tilted his head at me. "Ain't it too soon for you to be leavin' yo baby and shit?" I'm sure he didn't see the harm in his question, but instantly my heart tightened, and tears burned my eyes at the mention of the baby I'd lost. Most people who knew I was previously pregnant had enough sense not to ask, so I'd had yet to have a reason to say it out loud and I still wasn't ready.

"Fuck you!" choked up and pissed off at the same time, I snatched away and stormed off, leaving him standing there looking confused.

❧ 9 ❧

KANE

"Ugh, I see both yall niggas ain't got no manners!" the chick that Kendu was arguing with scoffed. "She lost her baby you asshole!" Instantly, I felt like shit for bringing up her shorty. I'd been surprised as fuck to even see her again after so long, and that was the first thing that came to mind. Once again I'd fucked around and put my foot in my mouth when it came to Makiyah. Ole' girl ran off behind her friend and it seemed like everybody got back to what they were doing except me and Kendu, who was still looking pissed off.

His ass had finally stopped talking about shorty, and I thought that meant he'd let his vendetta against her go, but obviously I'd been wrong. I was still stuck on me and Makiyah's interaction while he sat next to me, nursing a bottle of Hennessey and talking shit.

"Man that bitch, lucky all I did was snatch that nappy ass wig off her head! Up in here lyin' on my dick and shit. I ain't never had no complaints when I hit!" he grumbled, taking a sip of his drink and glowering down into the crowd below us.

"But according to her, you *didn't* hit." I told him, shaking my head as I poured myself some Dusse. As bad as I felt about what I'd said, I needed to shake it off because we were there for more than just partying. We had some business with Sean and had been totally thrown off by Kendu's bullshit.

"She fuckin' lyin'! Ain't no way I had her fine ass in a room and didn't fuck." He said with confidence, but the look on his face showed that he was trying to remember if that shit really happened or not. I couldn't believe that his ass had gotten too fucked up and left shorty hanging though. Actually, now that I'd heard her side of the story, it was even funnier that she took his weed.

"Apparently you did, and she took yo' shit as reimbursement. I think it was a fair trade though." I cracked, and he looked at me crazy as hell like he was ready to fight.

"Nigga fuck you!" He took another sip of his drink then checked the time. "Ain't we sposed to be meeting Sean or some shit?" The nigga thought he was slick trying to change the subject, but I'd let him make it for the moment since we did actually have business there.

"You lucky we need to head to his office, or I'd roast yo' ass, but I see this a touchy subject." I chuckled, unfazed by his attitude. "Bring yo' soft ass on."

"Yeah, ayite. Stop playin' with me bro!" He huffed, following my lead as I stood to my feet laughing, and we made our way out of the section and down a short hallway where Sean's office was located. I was feeling good about this meeting. Seeing how packed the club was, meant his ass should have our money. Giving the door a light tap, I pushed it open without waiting for him to say come in. He sat behind his desk with a shit eating grin until he saw me stepping inside, with Kendu right on my heels.

"What's up fellas? I wasn't expecting y'all in today." He chuckled nervously as I made my way further inside. Him saying that gained a snort from Kendu because we met every month like clockwork. I for real didn't know if niggas was just deciding to try me or what, but this was the second time our money had been played with. We still had yet to find any leads on who'd robbed our trap, and despite having already replaced the money I owed, I was still highly pissed about it. Usually, I was pretty chill and levelheaded, but if Sean was playing with my money too, he would feel my wrath.

"Sean, I know you ain't tellin' me you don't got my money right? I know that ain't what you sayin'?" I cut straight to the chase.

"Shiiit, that's what it sounds like to me bro." Kendu chimed.

"N-no no, nothing like that. I just need another week or two-." His words trailed off as I shook my head. Granted, it was only a measly ass twenty racks that he owed, but that mixed with my other recent loss had me feeling some type of way.

"You think we should wait a couple of weeks or take that shit in blood Du?" I asked, making Sean's eyes widen as he frantically looked between the two of us.

"Now you already know what I don't do *I owe you's.*" The sound of Kendu cocking his gun had a slow grin forming on my face just seeing the fear radiating off that nigga. He was already copping pleas, but I wasn't really trying to hear that shit.

"Look, look why don't I ummm." Sean's eyes bounced around looking for an escape, and trying to stall the inevitable.

"Gon' head bro-."

"Wait! I can sign my club over to you until I get the money! I swear you can even keep the profits as interest, just please don't kill me man!" He shrieked, cutting me off. I really hadn't planned on hearing him out. Honestly, I was just going to have Kendu hit him somewhere superficial and wait the two weeks, but his idea was much better.

"I think I'ma take you up on that. You got a pen?" I tugged at the hairs on my chin and asked. This nigga's eyes popped open, and surprise covered his face. Clearly, he hadn't expected me to agree so fast to his proposition, but it was too late to back out now.

"Uh, I need to have my lawyer-."

"Nah see you only got five minutes to run me yo' deed or

Kendu gon' drop yo' ass then I'll just sign the shit myself." I shrugged, and Kendu raised his gun for emphasis.

"Okay! Okay!" I watched him closely as he slowly climbed to his feet, careful not to make any sudden movements, and opened up a safe behind the huge self-portrait that sat on the wall.

"This nigga think he Scarface or some shit," Kendu grumbled beside me, but I never took my eyes off of Sean. I definitely didn't put it past him to try some slick shit. Scary niggas always tried to catch you off guard. I guess it was fortunate for him that he knew better, and exactly five minutes later, we were walking out of my new office with the deed in hand.

"Now nigga what the fuck you plan on doin' with a strip club with yo' petty ass?" Du wanted to know as we headed back to our section. Shit, it was no point in cutting our night short. If anything, I was ready to celebrate. A nigga had walked in expecting some chump change, but I was walking out a whole club owner.

Smirking, I shrugged because I hadn't even thought that far, but what I did know was that Sean wasn't getting shit back. At this point, the club was worth way more to me than the twenty bands he was late on. "Shiit, we gon' run this bitch and turn a profit!"

"Bet! First order of business is firing that lyin' ass thief! I'm bouta go do that shit now!"

"Man, hell naw! Let that girl be. You already done snatched her damn weave." I instantly yanked him back before he could walk off, and we both laughed.

"Fine then, I'm takin' my weed out her check tho!" He vowed, and I just shook my head at his slow ass. I already knew shit was going to be crazy with them two working so closely together, but I was going to do my best to keep them apart as much as I could. I'd worry about that later though because I planned to party for the rest of the night.

. . .

The next morning I woke up to a banging ass headache and my phone ringing loud as hell in my ear. Squinting against the sunlight, I reached for it just as it went silent and saw that it wasn't anywhere near as early as I thought it was. Before I could even get my bearings though, my phone was ringing again, and I already knew it wasn't nobody but my mama's ass. I always took her out for breakfast every Saturday, and I was running late as hell.

"My bad ma, I'm on my way now." It was the first thing out of my mouth when the call connected, but she was already huffing and puffing.

"No, your ass ain't! I can hear the sleep in your voice boy you probably ain't even out the bed yet!" She sucked her teeth and read my ass like a book as I swung my legs over the side of the bed. "How long it's gon' take you to get ready and really be on the way and don't be givin' me no weed man timeframe either!"

"Mannn what you know bout a weed man mama?"

"You in my business? Don't do that. Just bring yo' ass on!" I was still stuck on her saying that Meg Thee Stallion, hot girl shit when she hung up in my ear. My mama was grown as hell, so I knew she had her own life, but I was definitely going to talk to her old ass about what she was out there doing when Kendu or I wasn't around. Sighing, I shook off my drowsiness and went to handle my hygiene. After a piping hot shower and brushing my teeth, I got dressed quickly in a black t-shirt, some gray Nike basketball shorts, socks, and my smoke gray university six Jordan's. I planned on coming right back to the crib and getting a little more sleep before I hit the streets later on, so there was no point in putting on anything else. A half-hour later, I was headed towards my mama's crib, which wasn't nothing but a few blocks away. I'd barely pulled into the driveway of her five-bedroom, six-bath house, and she was stepping out onto the porch, dressed up and with not a hair out of place. I couldn't help smiling proudly at her dripped in the best because of us. If I didn't do nothing else with my life I'd make sure her shit was easy and filled with luxury because she definitely deserved it.

Our mama didn't look a day over thirty-five and half the time when we were out, people thought she was my woman and not the one that birthed me. As she descended her steps, I hopped out so I could open the car door for her since she had a frown on her face.

Smack!

"Don't be pullin' up on me late like I'm one of your lil' hoes Kane Malik Andrews!" She snapped, slapping me on the back of the head before turning around and kissing my cheek. Discreetly I rubbed the spot as she slid into the car and slammed the door. Her ass was going to be difficult, but I knew after she got some food in her, she'd be in a much better mood.

It didn't take us long to pull up to Yolk on Michigan Ave. Despite the time of day, I was pleased to see that it wasn't nearly as packed as I thought it would be. Off top I selected a table in the far back corner so that I could watch the comings and goings of everybody. As we made our way through the restaurant, I was stopped in my tracks by a familiar face.

Makiyah was looking good as hell and not at all like she'd been up until the wee hours of the morning working as she sat next to her son smiling and helping him color one of the little sheets. As soon as she saw me looking, she mugged the fuck out of me and rolled her eyes hard before putting her attention back on the paper. Chuckling at her attitude, I continued on to our table, glad that I'd picked the back, so I had the perfect view of her.

"What got you over there all smiley and shit?" My mama asked sipping on the Pepsi that the waitress had brought over after dropping off our menus.

"Whaaaat who smilin'? This just my normal everyday face." Lowering my eyes to the menu, I pretended to look it over even though I already knew what I wanted, just to avoid eye contact.

Regina Andrews had a way of seeing right through a muhfucka and would no doubt be able to smell my bullshit if I tried to lie.

"Mmmhmm. Let me find out you over there staring at that girl back there." She sucked her teeth. "She is pretty, but you gon' give her stalker vibes lookin' so hard and not speaking." Once again she'd called me out, and I couldn't do shit but laugh.

"Yooo chill ma, ain't nobody starin'." I lied, knowing damn well I couldn't take my eyes off of Makiyah.

"You the one that needs to 'chill.' Y'all swear y'all be gettin' over, just like Kendu's ass think I don't know about that lil' girl goin' around claimin' to be pregnant."

I hadn't heard that shit, and it immediately had me choking on my drink. "What? Who told you that?"

"Damn sure not you or your brother." She huffed. "I had to find out the old fashioned way......Facebook." She finally admitted with a shrug when I looked at her curiously. There was no way Kendu knew that some girl was blasting him on Facebook, but I was sure he was going to shit bricks when he found out. Just as quickly as she'd broached the topic, she was on to the next, and we continued talking until the waitress came and took our orders. The whole time I kept a close eye on Makiyah, we all ended up finishing at the same time. I made sure to have the waitress add her food onto mine, and my mama smirked like she knew some shit I didn't. "I'm goin' to the ladies' room. Speak to her and stop being so weird." She walked off just as Makiyah came stomping over with the same mean mug as before.

"I don't need you to buy me and my son nothin' okay! I'm not some charity case-!"

"I was just being nice shorty, you know extending an olive branch and shit since I never got the chance to apologize for what I said." I held my hands up. Surprised, her eyebrows shot up and she opened and closed her mouth a couple of times, unsure of what to say.

"Oh....well thank you." Her voice softened up a whole lot more.

"It's nothin'....what's up lil man?" Her son's head popped up, looking to her for approval, and when she gave him a small nod, he looked my way with a smile and waved shyly. "Yo daughter must be with her daddy today?" I asked, glancing back up at her after I gave little man some dap. It was hard not to look over her body in the tight ass biker shorts and t-shirt she had on. Her skin was glowing, and despite having just been pregnant, you'd never know it. Low key I was ready to say fuck my own rule and cuff her fine ass.

"Ummm, I don't have a .....do you mean my lil' cousin?"

"Oh damn, that's yo' cousin?" I didn't hide my surprise, and now I felt even worse about the assumptions I'd made about her.

"Yeah, that's my cousin Dymani's baby. I was just babysitting for her while she got sleep for work." She shrugged as her words trailed off.

"Oh shit, now you gotta let me take you out or something to make up for putting my foot in my mouth," I begged, and we shared a laugh while her son looked on in confusion.

"How about I let you know if we run into each other again." Her fine ass smirked. "Come on RJ, say bye." He happily waved as they walked off, leaving me salty as fuck.

"Come on shorty, that's how you feel?" My question was met with a shrug as she continued on out the door, making that ass sway without even trying. I nodded to myself because little did she know I would be running into her again much sooner than she thought.

❧ 10 ❧

KENDU

The song *Throat Baby* was playing on blast as I got some head in the front seat of my car. It was definitely the perfect song for the occasion, but more than anything, it's how I had been feeling ever since Ashlee sprung that baby shit on me. Just thinking about the possibility of being a father had my dick softening in shorty throat, and I got irritated all over again.

"Maybe it's because we in the car." Tae huffed, sitting up with drool hanging from her chin, instantly making my stomach turn. I wasn't no squeamish ass nigga or nothing, but Tae's ass was hit in the face, and she really looked like something out of a scary movie with that shit dripping down her face. Maybe it was just the expression on her shit, I didn't know, but I was definitely done with her ass. Her head game was A1 though, and the pussy was fake decent, but she was always a last resort. I'd popped up on her to try and relieve some pressure before I went and talked to Ashlee's stupid ass about this so-called pregnancy. Honestly, I planned to get ghost until I could hit her ass with a paternity test, but she'd been blowing me up and posting all types of shit on social media trying to get my attention. Unfortunately, my mama saw that shit before I did and insisted that I handle my business. She had that single mother's PTSD, so as soon as she peeped that I was denying what could be my baby, she got on my ass, and knowing my attitude, I was trying to be prepared and couldn't even do that.

Sighing, I stuffed my dick back into my jeans while Tae watched. The bitch still hadn't attempted to wipe her fucking mouth, and I had to look straight ahead so I wouldn't see that shit. "I ain't even got time for all that. I'm sposed to be at Ashlee's in a few- bruh wipe yo' fuckin' face man!" I snapped, unable to handle her just letting that shit sit on her face.

Unfazed by my tone she used the back of her hand to wipe her mouth grossing me out more. "Sooooorrry, but I thought you had already been there. She said y'all damn near live together." I could detect a slight attitude in her tone and couldn't do shit but shake my head. She and Ashlee were friends. Actually, they were best friends, so she was well aware that I was fucking shorty, but she never cared. Being the ugly friend out of the two, she was used to Ashlee getting all the attention and niggas, so being the insecure thirst bucket that she was, she always went out of her way to fuck the same niggas. And I wasn't any different. At first she was cool playing the background, but now she always turned her nose up whenever I mentioned Ashlee. I wasn't serious about either one of them, so I didn't care either way.

"She sounds stupid for tellin' you that shit, and you sound stupid for believing it." I griped. I wasn't trying to be the topic of discussion when them hoes got together, and I damn sure didn't appreciate being lied on. Ashlee knew what it was between us, or at least I thought she did. Obviously, I needed to check that shit, but how could I without letting her know that I was fucking her friend too.

"How I'm stupid when she was telling anybody who'll listen that she pregnant by you? I just thought you were tryna be a family man and shit." She said sounding even dumber than before.

"And you still came out here to suck yo' best friend's baby

daddy's dick. Bro get yo' ass out!" Now I was big mad, and I barely let her step out onto the sidewalk before I was peeling off. I hated a goofy bitch, and Tae had taken up all of the time I had to spare for one, so I definitely wasn't pulling up on her ass either.

Instead of heading out to her house, I detoured and went home to shower and change clothes. I needed a drink or two, and what better place to get one than our new club. At first I thought it was crazy for Kane to put more on our plate by taking Sean's shit, but it definitely made sense. Not only would we be getting what the nigga owed us plus interest, but I'd also be able to see shorty fine ass whenever I wanted. We'd decided to wait a few days before announcing to the staff that we were taking over, and I could just imagine the look on her face when she found out. After snatching her wig off, I wasn't even that mad about my weed anymore, and at this point, I really just wanted to see what the pussy was like. Good pussy was always attached to a crazy ass broad, and I hadn't met nobody as crazy as shorty.

Sparking up a blunt, I made the trip home in no time and hopped right in the shower. The three shower heads that I had installed in my luxury condo had definitely been worth the money and damn near had me ready to just call it a night. The chance to irritate old girl had me getting dressed and on my way to the club though.

Just like the night before it was packed, and everybody in there was turned the fuck up. I slid through that bitch dolo with my tool tucked into the front of my pants, not at all worried about a nigga trying me. Everybody had their eyes glued to the stage anyway as a stripper who put Buffy the Body to shame twerked to some City Girls track, so they definitely weren't paying me any attention. I made it to the only VIP section that was open and sat down waiting for one of the bottle girls to come take my order and smirked, seeing that it was exactly who I came to see that strolled up. As soon as she saw me sitting there, she rolled her eyes.

"I should've known it was yo' ass up here." She scoffed shaking her head, and I could see that she had a new wig on. It wasn't as long as the other one, but it touched the middle of her back and looked much more natural. "Helllllooo nigga! This section is already booked!" I had tuned out the shit she was saying as I scanned her body in the black cutoff tank top and matching booty shorts she was wearing.

"I got it now. Tell whoever it is they beat." I licked my lips and flashed her a dimpled grin, tossing a knot of bills out onto the table that I knew more than covered the section. Judging by the look on her face, she was mad as hell that they'd sent her to deal with me instead of someone else. She mumbled some shit I couldn't make out and snatched my money up.

"What you want?"

"Bring me a bottle of Hennessy," I said, pulling out my ringing phone and instantly hitting ignore at the sight of Ashlee's name on the screen.

"Ayite that's what had you getting ED last time. You better brace yourself big daddy." This was the second or third time she'd said that shit, and despite knowing that my dick worked just fine in normal circumstances, I had to wonder if maybe I had done her dirty. I definitely couldn't remember shit from that night after getting the room, so it was a possibility that I'd fallen asleep on her ass for real.

"Mannn, I wish you'd stop sayin' that shit. *If* and that's a big fuckin' if, my dick didn't wanna act right it was probably cause of yo' ass." I shrugged thinking she was about to go off, but she just laughed.

"Whatever help you sleep at night big daddy." She went to walk away, giving me a glimpse of her name printed on the back of her shirt and on some thirsty shit I ran behind her. *Dymani.* That shit definitely fit her to a T

"Aye Dymani!"

"What you want nigga?" She whipped around, snatching her hand out of mine.

"You say I did you dirty, right? Let me get a do-over?" I asked just as surprised by my request as she was, but it wasn't like I could let her keep walking around claiming I had ED. She was one of them females that wasn't going to ever let me live that shit down unless I redeemed myself, and I planned to do just that.

"Hell naw, you not bouta trick me again! Nope!" She was being difficult as hell even though I hadn't really expected her to agree right away. I wasn't in the mood to sit and beg.

"Maaaan." Once again, I grabbed her hand, holding on just a bit more firmly, and headed back towards Sean's old office. I had no clue if that nigga was in there, but I'd make his ass leave if he was.

"I know you better let me-!" She didn't get a chance to finish whatever she was about to say because I backed her into the wall and kissed her. Just from the way she talked, I knew her ass liked that rough shit. I wrapped my arms around her waist and palmed her fat ass. She pushed against my chest with a squeal that had her mouth opening slightly, and I slipped my tongue inside. The fight she was putting up, finally died and now she was pressing her body into mine and moaning as our tongue's explored each other's mouths.

Never breaking the kiss, I lifted her off her feet and carried her the rest of the short distance to the office. I could feel the heat radiating off her pussy through the thin ass shorts she had on. Shorty was more than hot and ready, and I really couldn't wait to dive in her shit.

As if God was rooting for me, the room was dark and empty. I quickly flipped the light switch on with my free hand and stepped all the way inside, carrying her over to the desk. Real shit, I rarely ever put my mouth on a female, but I had a point to prove with Dymani and on top of that, I actually wanted to see what her pussy tasted like. I put just enough space between us so I could remove her shorts and she squinted up at me evilly.

"You better make this worth it." She warned, leaning back

onto her elbows. I grinned confidently, already knowing I was about to have her ass climbing the walls in this bitch. Her shorts and thongs were off in one swift motion, giving me the perfect view of her pretty ass pussy. It was cleanly shaven and glistening like she'd just oiled that muhfucka up. I pulled my gun out and set it down on the desk beside her before lowering myself to the floor so that I was face to face with her clit. Shorty smelled like a whole fucking fruit salad, and I didn't waste any time sucking her lips into my mouth. I let my tongue snake its way up her opening, dipping briefly inside of her before focusing on her hard clit. We both moaned at the same time, me from how good her nectar tasted and her from the pleasure I was inflicting. She was so fucking wet that it sounded like a nigga was slurping noodles in that bitch, and I was lapping it all up.

"Ooooh fuck!" She whimpered, throwing her head back as I rapidly flicked my tongue before latching on to her pearl and sucking on it hard. "Ohhh! Ohhh I-I'm commmiiiing!" Her body shook violently as she tightened her legs around my damn head to the point that I almost couldn't breathe, but I just continued my assault on her pussy. I'd meant exactly what I said about redeeming myself, and by the time I was finished with her she'd be begging for the dick every time she saw me. She was still riding the high of her orgasm when another one had her back arching off the desk.

Licking her clean, I stood up and wiped her juices from my face while she attempted to get her bearings. My dick was already straining against my jeans, anticipating the feel of her walls and within seconds I'd kicked them bitches off and was standing before her completely naked. I silently thanked God that I hadn't wasted the condom I had on Tae's funny looking ass as I slipped it on and stepped between her open legs.

"I know yo' shit talkin' ass ain't bouta tap out from some head?" I teased raising an amused brow, and she sat up with her signature mean mug like I hadn't just had her quivering a second before.

"Don't brag it's usually the niggas that can't fuck that eat the best pussy."

I chuckled as she removed her tank to reveal her perky bra less titties with silver nipple rings I didn't even know she had, and my dick grew harder if that was possible. Since the desk was so high, I was positioned right at her opening, and I slid between her folds covering the condom in her juices before dipping my head in. She was already wincing from just the tip, letting me know her shit was probably tight as fuck.

Covering her lips with mine, I took her tongue and sucked it into my mouth as I eased my full length inside of her. "*Baby.*" I couldn't stop myself from groaning at the feel of her silky walls wrapped around my shit. With the way she had me in a choke-hold and the soft moan she let escape into my mouth, it was everything I could do not to nut right then.

I cupped one of her thick legs into the crook of my arm once the feeling subsided a little and began to grind into her slowly. Shit, I was barely five strokes in and was ready to unload in the condom, so I pulled out instantly, making her look at me crazy.

"Don't worry baby, I'm not takin' your dick away," I mumbled helping her down and onto her feet. "Bend yo' ass over." I slapped her on the booty making it jiggle, and she squealed sexily.

"Mmphm!" She laid across the desk with one leg raised so that ass was sitting up nicely giving me a glimpse of her pussy and I just had to stick my face back in there. I let her get close to coming again and abruptly slammed my dick in her. "Sssss, fuuuck!"

It was crazy how just the amount of pleasure I was giving her had me trying not to nut as I gripped her hip tightly with one hand and grabbed a handful of her hair with the other. I was surprised as fuck that bitch didn't slide off or that my fingers didn't get caught in any tracks, and that only had me going harder.

"Ohmygoooood!" I smirked at her words coming out jumbled and planted a quick kiss on her neck.

"Yeah, next time you mention this dick it better be with the upmost respect." I ordered slamming into her with a hard left stroke that had her clawing the desk.

"Ooookaaaaay! I'm coming baby! I'm commmmiiiing!"

"Man what the fuck!" Sean's voice sounded off behind me, but I felt my balls tingling and knew I was on the verge of busting a big ass nut, so I didn't even pause my movements.

"Get the fuck out! Now nigga!" I barked and the door slammed shut just as my kids came shooting into the condom. A nigga was tired as fuck after that, and I took my time sliding out of Dymani's wetness as I tried to catch my breath.

"Nigga you gon' get me fired!" Dymani wiggled away panting, clearly snapping out of her sex-induced haze.

"Yo' ass ain't getting fired bro." I sighed discarding the condom in the small trash can next to the desk. While she was bouncing around trying to clean up and get redressed I was taking my sweet ass time.

"Yeah Ayite! Sean might be scared of you but he don't give a damn about replacing me!" By now she'd shimmied her way back into her shorts and stood before me topless. I wrapped my arms around her and pulled her body into mine, looking down at her with lust-filled eyes. Her ass was so fucking pretty even when she looked like she was ready to kill my ass. I'd already made up in my mind that this shit between us wasn't going to be a one-time thing. She definitely had the type of sex I needed to put in rotation and I planned to do just that.

"You ain't gotta worry about Sean doin' shit. My brother and I got the deed on this bitch, so from now on, I'm boss man and big daddy to you baby." I admitted with my chest poked out. It didn't make no sense how good pussy could make you say shit you wasn't supposed to, but I'd deal with spilling the beans about our shit later.

❧ 11 ❧

DYMANI

A bitch was literally still having flashbacks of the dick that Kendu had delivered, and it had me missing him and hating his ass at the same time. After the first and second encounter with him, I figured his sex was mediocre at best and had no intentions on fucking him if given the opportunity, and now I was glad that I had. Well, I appreciated the much needed orgasm at the time, but now I was feigning for a nigga I knew couldn't be no good. It was obvious in the way he talked and acted that he wasn't shit and he damn sure wasn't the type I needed after dealing with Twan. Unfortunately, he had dope dick, and if it was true about him and his brother owning the club, then I didn't doubt I'd be dipping off with him every chance I got, just like Kya's dick dizzy ass had been doing with Sean.

My phone went off, snapping me out of my freaky thoughts, and I blew out an irritated breath at the sight of Twan's mama calling. I had no clue what she wanted, but I was sure it had to do with her son. I hadn't heard from him since he'd broken into my apartment, not even to check on Armani, and after his new get rich quick scheme, I could only assume his ass had gotten locked up.

Rolling my eyes, I answered dryly not even caring about whether she heard it or not. "Hey, Kim-."

"Ahhhhh my baaaaby!" Her screaming had me pulling the phone from my ear with a wince. She was crying so loud I couldn't even understand what she saying, and I started to hang up until I heard Twan and killed through her ramblings.

"Kim! Kim, slow down I-!"

"They just pulled Twan out of Lake Michigan! Somebody shot him!" She managed to get out, and my breath caught in my throat.

"I'm on my way!"

It took me over an hour to get Armani and myself dressed and across town to Kim's apartment, and the entire time I was praying that there had been some type of mistake. We may have been going through our little bullshit, but I didn't want the nigga dead and regardless of his recent absence he was still the only father that my baby knew. I was glad that she was such a heavy sleeper and hadn't woken up yet because I was a distraught mess. It may have been the fact that I'd just seen him or that we'd had words that night, but I just couldn't stop the tears streaming down my face. I kept trying to figure out how I was going to explain to a three-year-old that she'd never see her daddy again. It was just too much to handle at the moment, and I knew being around his family was just going to make it worse.

As soon as I pulled onto Kim's block, I could recognize a few of the cars parked out front, and a fresh wave of tears sprang from my eyes. Parking a little ways up the street I got myself together as best I could before taking Armani out of her seat and making the trip to the door.

Unfortunately, Kim's sister Maxine answered and gave me the nastiest look she could muster. "What are you doing here?" She spat, blocking my entrance like a bodyguard or something. Maxine had never liked me, and she'd made it clear from the first time that Twan brought me around. I never cared or concerned myself with whatever her issue was because Kim always welcomed me with open arms, so her bitter ass sister was the least of my worries. Usually I ignored her, but today was going to be the day I put her in her place with the way I was feeling.

"Kim called me." Was my only explanation as I brushed past her bumping her shoulder. I was daring her to say something crazy so I could beat her ass for old and new, but she merely sucked her teeth and walked off which was her best bet.

"Oh Dymani you made it!" Kim popped up out of nowhere and pulled me into a tight embrace. Just seeing her had me emotional again, and I clung to her small frame.

"Of course, no matter what we had going on, I loved Twan." I choked out relishing in the comfort she was providing.

"I know baby, I know." She affectionately cupped my cheek as she blinked back tears.

"D-did they say what happened? Do they know who did this?" I already had an idea that Twan's murder had something to do with some street shit. It was the only thing that made sense. He wasn't the type that had enemies, and for the most part, he stayed out of trouble.

Kim shook her head profusely and swallowed hard. "No, just that he was shot and obviously thrown in the lake. I don't even know who'd do some shit like this."

"The police are gonna find them Kim." I told her in an attempt to ease her mind some, even though the truth was that shit like this involving a black man was rarely solved.

"Tuh! You don't even believe that!" Maxine called herself saying lowly, but I heard her loud mouth ass and rolled my eyes her way. Either Kim didn't want to hear that or was choosing to ignore her stupid ass because she nodded with a sniffle and took Armani from my arms.

"Come on, I want you to meet some family." Grabbing my hand with her free one, she led me into the living room where I was introduced to cousins I hadn't yet met and reacquainted with his grandmother and a few others. I ended up sitting around with the family for a few hours, just talking and telling stories about Twan that had us laughing and crying. Everyone besides Maxine was really nice and enjoyed Armani even though that bitch kept making snide remarks. I kept it cute for Kim's sake and didn't haul off and slap her like I wanted to.

By the time I packed my baby away in the car to drive home, I'd calmed down a lot. I was still very much hurt but was no longer crying at least. I still hadn't decided how I'd tell Armani about Twan so I was just going to keep it to myself for a while. She was still amped after receiving a ton of attention and sweets at Kim's house, and I didn't want to bring her down by telling her such bad news. Instead I decided that we'd order a pizza and watch movies for the rest of the night.

"Wanna have a girl's night baby?" I asked glancing back at her through the rear view and she quickly nodded clapping her hands excitedly.

"Gworls night! Moona!"

"Oh naw, not Moana again Mani. Don't you wanna watch something else?" She made me watch Moana which was her favorite, over and over again. Like literally my grown ass knew every line and song in that movie, and I often tried to convince her to watch something else to no avail.

"Moona! Moona!" She began chanting, and I couldn't help but laugh at her little cute face. I didn't have a clue who Yancy had gotten pregnant by, but obviously her genes were so strong that she didn't have a trace of anyone else in her that I could tell. That's why it was so easy for people to accept when I said she was my daughter and not my sister. I was sure that if I was able to see them the same could be said for our brothers, but I hadn't seen them in more than a few years, and Yancy hadn't made a single attempt to get them back.

"Okay fine, we can watch Moana but next time I get to pick." I shook myself out of my thoughts and gave her a fake smile. She was still cheering when we made it back home, and as soon as we stepped in the door, she was running around. While she burned off her energy, I took the time to order our pizza with hot wings for me and once that was done I called Makiyah to let her know what happened with Twan. She was just as shocked as me and offered to come over, but I really just wanted to spend time alone with my baby. After spending the afternoon with his family, I definitely wasn't up for company. I promised we'd get together the next day for lunch and to take the kids out though.

Hanging up I went to run Armani some bath water and added just a little bubble bath. By the time she was done, the pizza had arrived and I set her up at the table while I went to take a shower of my own. Alone in the comfort of the hot shower, I allowed myself to be open for just a few minutes and cried my heart out. I cried for me, my baby and Twan, but once I finished I wiped my face and went out to eat pizza and watch Moana with Armani. Today was only the first day, and I knew I had a long way to go before I'd ever feel completely okay again, but until then, I was going to continue to take things one day at a time.

❧ 12 ❧

KANE

"Send me that info bro." I said to my man's Q and hung up at the sound of a knock on my door. I'd just gotten a tip on the niggas who'd robbed us, and I was ready to go act on it. Since taking over the club and dealing with all of the paperwork and permissions that I had to fill out just to get the dispensary up and running, I'd been busy as hell. The shit was a lot more work than I thought it'd be and way more expensive, which reminded me of the money I was out. We'd still been moving product with no issues. No other niggas trying to pop up with some new shit and no other hits, so I was positive that whoever had been dumb enough to break in our shit was laying low or had run their asses out of town. Because of Ricardo and the business I was in, I had connections all over, so I'd reached out to a few in some other big cities, and I was waiting on a word from one of them. In the meantime though, I'd keep my focus on moving my work, the club, dispensary and...Makiyah. Today was the day I was going to reveal that I was the club's new owner, and I couldn't wait to see the look on her face. She'd told me to wait until we ran into each other again, not even knowing that we'd be seeing each other every night she worked. It was bound to work out in my favor. "Come in!" I shouted, and the door slowly came open, revealing Kya standing there in her uniform. Sean had promoted her to some type of manager, so she was always around, and while she seemed like she handled her job smoothly, something about her ass just seemed off to me.

"Hey bossman, I just came to let you know I was finished stocking the bar and that the girls are starting to arrive." She switched over to my desk and leaned over it so that I could see her titties spilling out. "Is there *anything* else I can do for you?" The look on my face should've made it clear that I wasn't interested, but she didn't take the hint. She licked her glossy ass lips and flipped her hair as she awaited my response.

"Yeah, round up the girls, we'll be having a staff meeting in twenty minutes." Confusion flashed across her face but quickly disappeared, and she giggled.

"Noooo, I mean can I be of any *service* to you." She reiterated, walking around the desk so that she was standing over me, assaulting my nose with whatever cheap ass body spray her ass was wearing. "You know sometimes I'd help Sean relieve a lil' stress when shit got hectic in here. I could do the same thing for you." She reached out to touch me and I bent her damn hand back quick as hell, making her yelp loudly.

"I don't want that second-hand pussy. Get the fuck up outta here yo' ass fired, tryna sexually harass me!" I spat releasing her, and she damn near ran out the door whimpering. I felt dirty just having touched her nasty ass, and just as her words replayed in my head I jumped out of my chair fast as hell. My nose turned up looking around the office pissed off. Her and Sean had probably been fucking all over that muhfucka and I'd been sitting in there. Irritated I went and washed my hands, wishing I had time to go home and change my clothes too, but the club would be opening soon and I still needed to introduce myself to the staff. I made a mental note to get some new furniture in there as I locked it back up and headed downstairs to make sure Kya's ass was gone and round everybody up.

I guess I didn't have to though because when I reached the

first floor, all of the strippers and bottle girls were lined up in front of the bar with Kya and the other bartenders too. Almost immediately, my eyes locked with Makiyah's, and she balled her face up in confusion. I'd definitely be talking to her privately, but first, I had to handle some shit. The grin I gave her fell immediately, and I focused on Kya who was standing there like I hadn't just fired her.

"Fuck is you still doin' here? I wasn't playin', clear yo' shit out and beat it." I voiced giving her a hard stare. Her jaw dropped as the other girls started murmuring but made no move to do what I'd said.

"But I-!"

"Aye Big L!" I shouted for one of the bouncers and he appeared a second later, waiting on instructions. He and his crew were new hires I'd made to secure the club, so they already were aware of my position. "Escort her the fuck up outta here, and she's not allowed back, not even as a customer." A simple nod, and he was snatching her up while she screamed and fought.

"Fuck you! You can't ban me! I fuckin' run this club! Wait til Sean finds out!" I bit back a chuckle at the threat of Sean finding out. That nigga couldn't do shit with me and had no say-so over anything that happened at Eclipse. Shaking my head, I turned back to the other ladies to find them all staring back in disbelief.

"If you can't tell already, I'm the new owner Kane, along with my brother Kendu and whatever shit that nigga Sean was going for ain't gon' fly with me. Now I just took over, so I haven't sorted everything out yet, but there will be some changes around this muhfucka, and I hope that y'all can adjust cause if not, then you gon' find yourself unemployed just like Kya's ass." I shrugged indifferently, looking at each one of them. "Any questions?" Almost immediately this light skin girl's hand shot up.

"So is you raising the payout at the end of the night?" She asked and the other girls started mumbling to each other again. There wasn't much I knew about the behind-the-scenes of a strip club, so whether or not Sean had them paying too much or too little was beyond me.

"How much you payin' now?"

"Twenty percent, plus we each pay the dj a few dollars." The first thing that came to mind was how could Sean not have my money when he was taking that much of their shit every night? The nigga was clearly fucking off his money and didn't have shit to show for it.

"Naw I won't raise y'all shit for now," I told her, scratching the back of my head. I needed to get an accountant in there to look over his books, so I'd know if I even wanted to keep it at the twenty percent. It seemed steep especially considering if they hadn't had a good night. It turned out there were a lot of grievances they had, and I planned to address every one of them so that I could get the most out of taking over. I went over a few more things before dismissing them to go ahead and get ready for the night. As soon as they walked off, I made my way over to Makiyah, who was already in her spot behind the bar.

"So, you gon' let me take you out now? This our second time running into each other." I couldn't help letting a cocky smirk flash as I took a seat on one of the empty bar stools. Chuckling, she shook her head.

"Boooy, this definitely don't count as runnin' into me. Yo' ass probably had taken over the club when I said that shit." She called me out with a hand on her waist, and I had to laugh.

"Okay, you got me," I said holding my hands up. "but in my defense it's definitely worth it." I was on some straight thirsty shit, ready to ask her ass every day until she agreed, just to spend some time with her. At first, it was really all about making up for the shit I'd said to her, but now I wanted to get to know her. She'd obviously been through a lot and was still managing to put on a brave face for her son. There'd never been a time I could remember wanting to know everything about a female. Like what she liked and disliked, her goals and shit, especially if she had kids. Being who I was bitches always flocked to me, so I never had to chase and there was never any need for a conversation outside of where we'd meet to fuck. I was completely out of my element with Makiyah, but it wasn't going to stop me from trying.

"Well I don't think it'd be a good idea, especially with you being my new boss now." She quipped raising a brow.

"Maaaan, you gon' try to throw that shit up in my face?" I feigned shock loving the way she looked when she smiled.

"That's a big deal though."

"Girl, I'll sign this shit over to my brother right now! What about then?" My persistence had her laughing loudly, which drew the other bartender's attention whose name I hadn't learned yet. "See you got me down here embarrassing myself begging and shit. I'm just tryna feed you or something, no strings attached." I watched a series of different expressions wash over her face as she considered it and didn't even realize that I was holding my breath until she finally sighed.

"Ok fine, one dinner, but I don't want you treating me any differently as far as work, whether we have a good time or not." She tried to give me a stern look that was more cute than intimidating.

"I got you. I'm gon' treat you just like everybody else around here, even though I know you definitely gon' have fun with a nigga. Deal?" I stuck my hand out so we could shake on it on some corny shit smiling when she stuck her soft hand in mine.

"Deal." Just from how hesitant she was to agree I knew she was probably worried as fuck about taking it there with me, but I was definitely going to make sure she didn't regret giving me a chance.

❧ 13 ❧

MAKIYAH

It was finally the day of my date with Kane, and I was nervous as hell. I wasn't used to niggas wanting me and actually taking action to spend time with me the way he had. It made me question his intentions and wonder what he wanted with me. I'd barely gotten over what Romell had put me through, and I didn't think I was prepared to deal with more heartache.

"Stop looking so damn mean! You're messing up my makeup!" Dymani growled, rubbing a brush over my face. Despite what she was going through, she'd insisted that I let her help me get ready, and she was way too excited for me to say no. For some reason she liked Kane for me apparently and thought it was cute that he'd asked me out. Considering how intuitive she was I tried not to stress too much over the possibility of him being anything like my baby daddy. Romell had done a number on me, and I was leery of opening up to anybody of the opposite sex.

"Sorry, I'm just nervous as hell."

"We'll don't be. You gon' look sexy as hell, and you better act like it too." She scolded. "Now go put on your dress so you can see the finished product."

I'd given Dymani full reign over my entire look for the night so the outfit, hair, and makeup had been all up to her, and that had me nervous too. It looked like a simple black bodycon dress until I went into my bedroom and slipped it on. The front was sheer and showed straight through to my bra and panties in a criss-cross design that made it not as revealing as it could've been. The heels she'd laid out for me were black and open-toed, displaying my white polished toes and adding a good four inches to my height. After putting everything on, I just knew that I looked different without looking in the mirror, but I wasn't prepared for the transformation that Dymani had put me through.

A bitch almost cried when I stepped into view of the full-length mirror. My braids were out, and Dymani had flat ironed my hair to perfection with a part down the middle. She'd given me a light beat with a Smokey eye and red ombré lips that had me looking like I'd just done a photoshoot in a magazine, and coupled with the dress and heels I was like a whole new person. Even my body was popping, and I couldn't stop turning side to side as I stared at myself in awe.

"Open up bitch, I can hear you in there overthinking!" Dymani knocked before storming into the room. "Ohhh shit, I did that!" She bragged loudly snapping her fingers when she saw me still standing in front of the mirror. I looked on bashfully as she circled me, squealing until she shouted that she needed to take some pictures. Before I could object, she was out of the room and returning with her phone in hand. She directed me to make a few different poses, gassing me up the whole time like a proud mama and after a minute or so, I felt confident enough to really get into it.

It'd been a long time since I'd been able to get dolled up completely. Spending all of my money on food and bills had drained my pockets in the past, and outside of things for Rj, I never had any money left over for extras. Then with Romell and his constant bullshit my confidence level had reached zero. I may have put myself together whenever I left the house but I never felt good enough or like I was deserving of any compliments. Since he'd left I had been working to build myself back up though. Healing myself from the inside out, and even though it was a slow process, I was getting there.

That was part of the reason why I'd decided to take Kane up on his offer for a date. I needed to learn to accept being treated well, and besides that, I hadn't been taken out in a long time. Why shouldn't I get a free meal and hopefully enjoy the company of a man that thought I was attractive? Hopefully, he wasn't as rude as he was the first couple of times that we'd been around each other.

"Oooh, I'm bouta post these right now!" Dymani's loud ass beamed, snapping me out of my thoughts.

"Oh lord."

"Oh lord is right biiiiiitch! That's exactly what that nigga gon' say when he pull up and see you lookin' like a whole buffet! I'm probably gon' get a promotion for this shit so make sure you tell him this is all courtesy of Dymani!" She was dead ass serious too, and I couldn't help but laugh just as a loud knock sounded at my door.

"He's here!" suddenly, I was a ball of nerves again and unsure of what to do. I spun around in a circle looking for nothing in particular while Dymani stood watching me with her brows raised.

"First of all, calm down. You were *expecting* him." She said slowly, rolling her eyes like I was retarded or something. Without another word she left the room, and I could hear her letting him in while I tried to get myself together. Already doubts were creeping in, telling me that I shouldn't be going out so soon after losing the baby and Romell, that I was being a hoe for even being in a new nigga face, and what would people think. I literally had to talk myself back down because the truth was it had been over a month since I'd miscarried, and Romell hadn't even been there for me the entire time I was pregnant and not at all when I'd lost the baby. It was time that I stopped thinking about him and started putting myself first.....well second after RJ.

"Ky! Yo' date here!" Dymani yelled from the living room, and I damn near jumped out of my skin. After another quick once over in the mirror, I smoothed down my hair and grabbed my clutch. His cologne hit me before I even rounded the corner and my knees got weak. The scent was manly and woodsy and probably expensive as hell, but most importantly, it already had me swooning.

"Damn, you look.....gorgeous." he complimented gazing at me from across the room, while Dymani looked on cheesing with her crazy ass.

"Thank you." I felt my cheeks heating and butterflies swarming my belly from the way he was drinking me in with his eyes, and I took a moment to appreciate how nice he looked. He was dressed in a black Balenciaga short sleeve shirt, jeans, and all-black Balenciaga speed sneakers. The only jewelry he wore was a pair of simple diamond studs, a thick diamond-encrusted Cuban link that rested against his broad chest and a matching watch, all of which was blinding. He looked completely out of place in my small ass living room filled with second-hand furniture, and I couldn't help but wonder if he'd look just as unmatched with me.

"You ready? I made us reservations, so we need to get goin'." He finally spoke, reaching out a hand to me that I reluctantly took with a nod.

"Okaaaay! That's what I'm talkin'!" Dymani cheered, making Kane smirk as we walked out the door. "Have fun and don't do nothin' I wouldn't do!"

I was glad when the door closed behind us, muffling whatever else her crazy ass was saying. I was already anxious enough without her extraness. "Have you ever been to Ruth Chris?" he asked, giving my hand a light squeeze. I was sure he felt how sweaty my palm was, but he still held on firmly, sending a shudder down my spine.

"Umm no."

"Good, the steaks there are bomb as fuck. They damn near melt in your mouth."

He continued to tell me about how good their food was as he led me out to his car, and I tried to act unfazed by how nice it was. Like a true gentleman, he opened the door and helped me inside before rounding the front and climbing in too. I remained tightlipped unsure of what to say as he started it up, and DVSN started playing softly, making me snap my head in his direction.

"What, you don't like them?" his brows dipped in worry. It was cute as hell, and I couldn't help but chuckle.

"I like them. I'm just surprised that *you're* listening to them." I explained and his face relaxed as he shrugged.

"I'ma keep it a buck, I only put this shit on for you.....but I can fuck with it." He flashed his perfect white teeth at me and pulled off. And there went those damn butterflies again. I was trying my hardest not to read too much into things, but I could definitely get used to being treated like... a lady.

The entire drive he held my hand over the console, occasionally rubbing my palm with his thumb as we made small talk. By the time we made it to the restaurant, I was a lot less relaxed until we sat down and I looked at the menu. My eyes damn near popped out of my head at the entrée prices alone. I tried to hide my shock, not wanting to seem like I wasn't used to shit, but I had definitely never been anywhere as expensive.

The waitress came and was talking, and thankfully Kane took the liberty of ordering us a bottle of wine and an Old Fashion for himself since I didn't recognize not one of the drinks on the menu. After bringing us our drinks, water and some warm bread, she disappeared leaving us alone. My ass read that menu front to back, and the cheapest thing I could find was some damn sparkling water. I must have been taking a long time because eventually, he asked if I knew what I wanted and I rapidly shook my head no.

"You know how expensive this stuff is?" I leaned over and tried to say in a hushed tone making him laugh.

"Baby girl, you're out with a boss. If you wanted to order everything on this menu just to taste it you can." He winked, and I swore my panties were going to need to be wrung out. I ended up ordering a T-bone since he swore by them with a side of mashed potatoes and asparagus, while he ordered the New York strip with the same sides.

By the time we'd finished eating, I was full, slightly light-headed, and even more attracted to Kane after learning more about him. I loved how much he respected his mama and how smart he was when it came to business. He gave me straight grown man vibes, and it was refreshing, which had me opening up about my own goals of becoming an author that I hadn't been able to see through. I'd even slipped up and told him some things about my situation with Romell without giving away too many personal details, which wasn't like me at all. He was just that easy to talk to, and I quickly realized that the same nigga who'd been rude as hell before had me open after a meal and one semi-deep conversation. I was definitely going to have to put some distance between us or I'd find myself in the same situation as before.

14

KENDU

"Did somebody named Twan work for you?" Dymani asked out of the blue, and my body instantly went rigid. We'd just finished cleaning up after a quickie in my new office and were putting our clothes back on. It seemed like she had crack in her pussy because I couldn't leave her alone and whenever I got the chance, I was pulling her in here. I wasn't ready to wife her or nothing, but I was definitely fond of her ass, and she'd just completely thrown me off. In all my years of living, I'd never been at a loss for words, but her mentioning that fuck nigga Twan had my tongue tied like a muthafucka.

"You askin' me about another nigga?" I stalled as a million thoughts went through my mind. Like how the fuck did she know his ass? Did she know anything about the robbery? Why was she even asking about him anyway? My first instinct was to immediately assume the worst and put a bullet in her head, but I was trying to work on my temper. She sucked her teeth as she finished putting on the last piece of her new uniform.

"I'm askin' about my baby's father." She rolled her eyes and my heart started pounding. That had been the last thing I thought was going to come out of her mouth. All the fucking we'd been doing we hadn't shared a bit of personal information, and I'd never considered asking her about her baby daddy. Now she was telling me it was the same nigga we'd murked a few weeks back, and I was feeling a mix of emotions. When I still hadn't said anything, she sighed again. "I'm just askin' because he told me he was working for GMM, and a few weeks later, he's being pulled out of Lake Michigan."

The fact that she wasn't looking at me suspiciously, made me relax just a little bit, but I still didn't need her sniffing around the GMM over that nigga. I was definitely going to kill the little muthafuckas that were given the task of disposing of him because he wasn't supposed to be found after that, and now I was dealing with this shit. Frowning as if I was trying to think, I repeated his name out loud.

"Twan, nah, I ain't never heard of that nigga, and I know everybody in my shit." I shrugged dismissively, not liking the look of sadness that washed over her face. It was no secret that bitches were always pressed behind their baby daddies, but I couldn't shake the jealousy I felt over her mourning him. I finished buttoning up my jeans and leaned up against the sink pulling her body into mine. "I'm sorry for your loss though. That shit is fucked up for real."

"It's cool. It figures his ass was lyin'." She chuckled bitterly. "Knowing him, he got mixed up in some bullshit the way he was flashin' money around." That had my ears perking up. He could've had money from working at the house, but I still felt like he had something to do with our trap being run up in. Now wasn't the time to ask her more about it though, so instead I captured her lips with mine.

"Don't worry about that shit, matter fact, let me take you and lil' mama out tomorrow." I surprised myself and said. Daytime outings was shit I didn't do, and now I was offering and throwing a kid in the mix. It was crazy what a little bit of guilt would have you doing. Her face instantly lit up though, and she batted those long ass lashes in my face.

"Awww, look at you tryna be nice. The funeral is tomorrow

though, maybe we can go another day." she offered, pecking at my lips. To say I was salty was an understatement, but I knew that she had to go pay her final respects to that bitch ass nigga, so I kept my cool.

"Whenever you want shorty." Satisfied, she kissed me again before running off to return to her post while I tried to figure out what the fuck I was doing. I'd never had no pussy that had me switching up, but it was obvious Dymani was more than just pussy. Plus, I felt somewhat bad about making her a single mother and taking away her daughter's daddy, even though he was a bitch. I didn't have time to dwell on the shit though, because Kane wanted to check out a lead Q had given him.

I found that nigga down at the bar in Makiyah's face like she didn't have a line of niggas waiting on drinks. It had only been a week, and I could already tell his nose was wide open, just seeing his ass over there showing all of his teeth from how hard he was grinning at her. He tried to straighten up when he noticed me standing beside him, but it was already too late.

"Wassup Ky?" I cheesed, and she gave me a shy wave, while Kane's ass grumbled under his breath.

"Hey Kendu." As quiet and bashful as she was it was hard to believe that her and Dymani were related, but I was sure people thought the same thing about me and my brother, so I couldn't even say shit. Besides, I liked Makiyah, she wasn't extra and she stayed to herself, which was exactly the type of female Kane needed after his ratchet ass ex.

"Aye, we gotta go do that thing." I nudged him and we locked eyes, silently communicating.

"Oh yeah, I forgot about that shit. Give me a second, I'll meet you at the car." He tugged at that raggedy ass beard and put his attention back on Makiyah.

"Bet.....ole sprung ass nigga." I mumbled the last part as I walked off. It took a whole ten minutes before he finally emerged from the club, looking all giddy and shit. I'd already rolled up and started smoking while I waited on his ass, and I quickly passed it off to him once we both climbed in the car.

"Q said he was sure about this shit?" I raised a brow as I prepared my gun with a silencer. Since we were going to our target, it was mandatory that we kept shit quiet. We definitely didn't want a neighbor or somebody hearing us and calling the police. Blowing smoke out of his nose, Kane gave me a dry-ass look and handed my weed back.

"Duh muhfucka." He clearly had an attitude like I was literally the reason he had to leave or some shit, but I didn't give a fuck. I was just trying to make sure since this was the first lead we'd gotten since we murked them niggas.

"Calm yo' buff ass down we gon' be back before yo' girl get off." I chided thinking of how funny it was that his ass was so pressed behind somebody baby mama, which instantly reminded me of my situation. "oh shit, speakin' of which, why I just find out Twan was Dymani's baby daddy." He'd been focused on the road, but his head quickly snapped in my direction.

"What? You think she was involved in that shit?" it was a legit question, and one I'd literally just asked myself, but something about it coming from him had me hot. I shook my head with dipped brows and tossed the rest of my blunt out of the window.

"Hell nah! You think she'd still be workin' at the club if she was? Besides, she would've known something was up weeks ago if she was that deep in it." I pointed out. It definitely didn't make sense for her to have been involved and I didn't believe that she was. "what nigga?" Kane was smirking at me like the damn joker and shit as he continued to whip through the busy streets.

"You like her ass, that's what."

"Maaaan, just cause you over there ready to wife Makiyah don't mean I like shit! Shorty cool, and the pussy good, but it ain't shit more than that." I lied making him bust out laughing.

"Don't be tryna throw me up in that shit, I can admit when I fuck with somebody! Yo' ass in denial though." I wasn't trying to hear that shit. I waved his ass off and cut the volume up on his radio, ignoring the way he chuckled and shook his head at me. Like I'd said Dymani was cool, but I wasn't ready to admit that I liked her ass. Shit, I don't think I'd liked anybody since my ass was in like grammar school or something. Once we started seeing real money, we saw that hoes were thirsty and willing to do anything to get close to us, which made me not really trust them. For the longest I only considered females as pussy, because what else did I need them for. In our business, it was stupid to confide in a bitch, so I didn't need a listening ear, especially since I had my brother. I was stingy with my paper, so I wasn't trying to share that, and I damn sure didn't want any kids. Besides this dick, there wasn't nothing I could even offer a female except now I was ready to offer Dymani my time. I wasn't telling Kane's ass that. Besides, I'd only really offered because of guilt....I think.

My phone started ringing back-to-back as we pulled into the dimly lit alley, and I cut that shit right off. It wasn't nobody but Ashlee's emotional ass, and I didn't have the time to argue with her. I still hadn't stopped by yet, and I knew that's what she was calling about, but she'd just have to wait until I felt like it. Stuffing my phone down into my pocket, I followed Kane out of the car and pulled on my ski mask while he did the same. After giving me a nod he crept through the gate with me right behind him and approached the dark house. It was obvious that nobody was awake inside, and that worked out perfectly for us.

Within minutes we'd picked the lock and were making our way through the kitchen guns in hand. Each of the two bedrooms we checked were empty, and so was the bathroom. We ended up finding the person we were looking for knocked out on the couch and I wasted no time kicking him in the leg.

"W-what the fuck is this? Who is you niggas?" he sat up, looking between Kane and me with horror all over his face.

"I'm the boogey man muhfucka! Where yo' bitch ass son?" I

grit, pressing my gun into his forehead, but Kane put a hand on my arm, and shook his head.

"Chill bro!"

Through the light from the tv, I could see his hard ass glare, and I backed off sucking my teeth in frustration, which made me even more irritated because that was a bitch trait. His ass was always telling me to chill when it was drill time! Swallowing my anger, I back up off dude, but kept my gun trained on him as Kane took over.

"Look, I-I don't know where that boy at! He and that nigga Ro, got into some shit, but he wouldn't tell me what, and the next thing I know he talkin' 'bout leavin' town! I ain't got shit to do with nothin'!" the man pleaded as tears streamed down his face. I guessed that was supposed to make his story more believable, but it didn't move me at all. The whole reason we were even there was because his ass had let it slip to the wrong person that his son was sitting on weight and since Noah wasn't a known player in the game that shit was a red flag. I bit down on my back teeth and tried not to let my pistol do the talking for me as he sat damn near hyperventilating.

"Y'all got some relatives outside the city that he'd go to?" Kane's old logical ass asked, and that nigga got to stuttering. "Listen, I ain't tryna hurt yo' people, I just want my shit back." his ass was lying through his teeth. Just for the running around we were doing I wanted to kill them niggas and I would. Hearing that nobody was going to be harmed calmed him down a little bit, but he was still looking at us suspiciously as he said.

"His mama got a sister out in Miami, but she not with all that street shit. She put her own sons out because they were joining gangs and selling drugs."

"Ayite....one more question and then we gon'." Kane lied again. "You said he was with a nigga named Ro? What you know 'bout him?"

"Uhh, his real name is Romeo, or Rome or some shit like that. He never really talked too much, but Noah told me he got a baby mama that he was taking with him." he nodded, eager to help so that we'd get the fuck out of his crib. Kane and I shared a look that meant I could go ahead and put his ass out of his misery. Without any warning, I shot him once in the neck and once in the head, making him fall backwards and his head slump to his chest.

After he'd taken his last breath, we set the house on fire with a bottle of Paul Masson that was on the floor next to the couch and dipped right back out the same way we'd come in. We'd found out a whole lot from dude's old snitching ass, and now the search was narrowed down to Miami. Ricardo had given us plenty of connections, and it wouldn't take shit to make a phone call and have niggas out there looking for a new crew in town. It was only a matter of time before I'd get to handle them niggas, and I couldn't wait.

❧ 15 ❧

DYMANI

Twan's funeral had been an entire mess, and I was feeling stupid for taking my ass in there with my baby. If it hadn't been for Makiyah being with me for support, I probably would've torn that damn church up! Not only was Maxine showing her ass, but at least five bitches popped up claiming to be that nigga's woman. It was like even from the grave he had me fucked up, and they were all lucky I didn't knock his ass out the casket.

I was glad that Armani was too small to know what the fuck was going on. She spent the entire time with her face glued to my phone along with RJ, oblivious to the chaos happening around her. Whoever had invented Peppa Pig was a genius for real.

"Why you still layin' down, ain't Du bouta be over there soon?" Makiyah's nosy ass asked, and I rolled my eyes at my phone screen.

"Girl, yo' ass swear you part of the family now, callin' him Du and shit." I grumbled sending her into a fit of laughter as I climbed off the bed to get ready.

"Why I gotta think I'm part of the family? Shit, if that was the case then Kendu thinks he's part of ours cause that nigga

called me Ky the other day. I wonder where he got that from?"
she gave me a pointed look, and although I was slightly irritated,
I couldn't stop the butterflies from forming at Kendu using my
nickname for her. Knowing the type of nigga he was I'd tried to
keep things between us on a strictly sexual level, which should
have been easy considering my hectic ass life at the moment.
He'd really thrown me way off though volunteering to spend
time with me and Armani. It didn't seem like something he
normally did and it had a piece of the wall around my heart chip-
ping away, which I hated because I knew he wasn't shit. And
after the fiasco at the funeral, I definitely wasn't trying to get
embarrassed by another nigga.

There was no doubt if I spent time with him outside of our
usual hookups, I'd fuck around and develop real feelings for him.
That wouldn't be good for either of us, because when my feelings
were involved, I was a completely different bitch.

"If he even called you that, it's not cause of me hoe." I
denied, with a shrug. "Ky just makes sense as a nickname for
you."

"Bitch, please! Nobody calls me that shit but yo' ass!" I didn't
appreciate her calling me out on my bullshit and I halfway
wanted to hang up in her face.

"Whatever!" I huffed, holding my phone in one hand while I
flipped through my closet, looking for something to wear with
the other. Kendu hadn't told me where we were going, but it was
safe to assume it'd be kid-friendly since Armani was tagging
along, so I needed something casual that was still cute. It took
me no time to settle on a pair of khaki, tight-fitting overalls that
scrunched at the ankle, a white spaghetti-strapped crop top and
my Coconut Air Max 97's.

I could already tell how good everything would look once I
put it all together. If I couldn't do nothing else I could definitely
put a look together, which was why I wanted to own my own
clothing store that offered style consulting. Never having shit
had made me really interested in fashion, and as a little girl I

loved looking through magazines at all the different outfits and study their makeup and hair.

It seemed like after they took my brothers and me from Yancy I was constantly struggling, and then she dropped off Armani with me. Taking care of a baby changed my goals and my focus shifted from opening up a boutique to providing for her. I'd never say that I regretted taking her in, but it had my plans on the back burner for a while.

"I'm gon' call you back, my other line ringing," Makiyah said, bringing me back to the present. "And you better be dressed by then too!" she hung up before I could even speak. Shaking my head I tossed my phone on the bed and went to get in the shower.

In no time I was dressed, and had thrown my natural hair into two French braids. I kept it simple with just some lip gloss on my full lips and some gold accessories. Once I was finished, I woke Armani up from her nap and put her on a cute pale pink Adidas short set with the matching shoes. I'd just braided her hair earlier in the week in preparation for the funeral so after adding a pink bow we were both ready.

Since I didn't know whether or not we were going to have food wherever we were going, I sat her at the table with a crustable sandwich and a Capri sun, before sitting down to wait for Kendu. He'd said he would be by at about five, and at ten minutes to the hour, he was texting to let me know that he was there, and my forehead bunched. I was going to have to remember that he wasn't his brother, so all that coming up to get me and opening up doors shit was going to be something I didn't get fucking with Kendu.

Sighing I quickly wiped Armani down and grabbed my little chain crossbody, Armani's backpack and her sippy cup before helping her out into the hallway. Her little inquisitive ass was asking a million questions the whole way, and I tried my best to answer each one. I scanned the block looking for Kendu's Jeep Renegade, until I saw it parked right behind my car, which was perfect for me since I still had to get her seat switched over.

As we made our way over Kendu climbed out with a big ass smile and my attitude melted away. "Damn you fine as hell." He complimented, stepping onto the curb and giving me a tight hug. As usual, he looked and smelled heavenly, dressed in a plain white Champion, t-shirt, some dark blue Levi's that fit just right and a fresh out of the box pair of Jordan Retro's. His neck, wrist, and ears were iced out, and he must've just hopped out of the barber's chair with how crispy his lining was. A bitch had to squeeze my legs together just to control the thumping in my clit, as his hands fell to the small of my back and he pressed a kiss into my neck.

Pulling away, he knelt down to where Armani was standing giving him the screw face. She definitely had my attitude and didn't fuck with too many people, which I loved. If Kendu wanted to get on her good side he'd have to work for it, because that charming shit wasn't going to work on her.

"What's up lil' mama, my name's Kendu but my people call me Du. What's yo' name?" he surprised me by extending a hand to her and I was even more shocked when she accepted it.

"My name Armani!" she damn near shouted, and Kendu looked up at me clearly pleased with himself.

"That's a pretty ass- I mean, that's a pretty name, Mani'."

"No! My name Armani, Doo doo!" her little face was once again balled up and I couldn't help but laugh at the way his brows dipped from her calling him doo doo.

"Nah, it's just Du-."

"Doo doo! Doo doo!" she was definitely getting a kick out of adding an extra Du to his name, and he looked up at me for help, but it wasn't shit I could do. His ass was going to forever be called Doo doo messing around with Ms. Armani. Shrugging, I held my hands up because he was on his own with that shit, besides if I tried to correct her she'd just be more adamant about saying it.

"Maaaaan, you got that lil' mama." He conceded finally standing back up with a pout that rivaled both Armani and Rj. "yall ready to go?"

"Yep, I just gotta grab her car seat....Doo doo."

"Get yo' ass..." he lurched like he was going to grab me, but I rushed off to my car to grab Armani's seat before he could laughing the whole way. By the time I got it out and came back, the two of them were engaged in a whole conversation. It was cute as hell seeing him interact with her, and I had to shake off the warm feeling it gave me. I distracted myself by strapping her chair into his truck, and once I was finished, I buckled her into it.

"You gon' tell me where we goin'?" I asked after we had finally pulled off and they'd taken a break in their conversation.

"Nope." He grinned and I feigned an attitude even though I was cheesing on the inside. This was a completely different side to Kendu and I had to admit that I liked it. He was smiling a whole lot and didn't seem as serious and straight forward. "ahhh yo' ass mad?" he teased, deep dimples showing.

"Nope."

"Lyin' ass. It's cool you gone like it though." He was super confident and that had me curious as hell, considering that his ass didn't know shit about kids. When he pulled up to the Chuck E. Cheese in Riverpoint center, I cracked up laughing.

"Chuck E. Cheese's!" Armani peeped the sign and immediately started clapping. This was one of her favorite places outside of the zoo, so he'd definitely won some points in her book.

"You ready for this lil' mama?" he wanted to know glancing into the rearview as he parked.

"Yeah!"

"Bet." He ended up being the one to unhook her car seat and carried her inside while I walked behind them. I didn't think anything of the lack of people around until we entered the play area and were the only ones in there.

"Why ain't nobody else here Kendu?" I asked, rolling my eyes because I already knew why. I just wanted to hear him say it and his ass barely looked up from the token machine where he was loading her a card.

"Cause I paid for just us to be here. I ain't tryna fuck no kid up for doin' somethin' I don't like to lil' mama, so I eliminated the issue." He shrugged like what he said made perfect sense and continued to add money to the machine. Armani stood beside him, getting more and more antsy as she watched, and I just knew she was about to bounce right out of her skin. It felt good to see her so excited after the week we'd had, so I wasn't going to fuck up her fun by telling him not to spend so much. Instead, I went and got us some pizza with a salad and drink.

I'd only been sitting there eating for about ten minutes when he brought his ass back with Armani skipping behind him holding a fist full of tickets. "Stop hiding and come get yo' ass kicked in some of these games." He leaned over me and said with those damn dimples on full display, and for the second time that day I was squeezing my thighs together.

"Come play mommy!" Armani chimed in, pulling at my arm and I reluctantly stood still chewing.

"Fine, but only a couple."

A couple of games turned into us playing everything in there at least twenty times. They even had Chuck E. come out and do the ticket dance, which we definitely didn't need since we had a whole pile stashed in a garbage bag nearby, but that didn't stop us from taking those too.

They never even got the chance to eat anything since we spent the whole three hours there playing, and by the time we cashed in our tickets, and Armani picked out one of each item, she was screaming for Chick-fil-A. Of course, her Doo doo was all too willing to get her some, but her ass was so tired that she barely made it through her little meal before she was knocked out snoring in the back seat. When he finally pulled back up to my crib and helped me carry everything up I was disappointed as fuck that he headed to the door immediately after. Shit, the whole day I'd been trying to keep my pussy in check and now that Armani was sleeping I just knew I was getting some dick.

"We should do this again, with and without lil' mama." he held my chin between his fingers and said as we stood in the open doorway. Unable to speak I merely nodded, making him grin before giving me a quick kiss and disappearing out of the door. The way my heart was beating as I watched him leave let me know that I'd fucked up and got feelings for my sneaky link.

🌿 16 🌿

KANE

"So, the whole building just gon' be full of weed?" my mama asked looking around in confusion as we walked through my building, and I shook my head with a chuckle.

"I mean it's gon' be some other shit in here, like edibles and bongs and shit like that, but for the most part its gon' be weed."

"Yeeeeah boy!" Kendu exclaimed slapping hands with me. He was even more geeked about this spot than he was the club and I could definitely understand why, with his weed loving ass. I'd finally gotten everything filled out and approved, so we were ready to start the construction. It wasn't much that we needed to get done so it wouldn't be long before we were able to start growing.

"I hope you're as excited about that baby as you are this weed." My mama was quick to check his ass and he balled his face up irritably. She'd been on his ass about Ashlee and the baby since she'd found out, and the fact that he had yet to go see about shorty didn't sit right with her.

"I wished you'd stop bringin' that hoe up bro-." she quickly slapped his ass on the back of the head.

"Don't call her no hoe, that's possibly the mother of yo' child! And don't call me bro!"

93

"Get yo' mama man she trippin'." Kendu mugged, rubbing his head where she'd hit him, but I quickly threw my hands up. I didn't want none of the energy she was giving his ass so I was staying out of it.

"Hell nah, that's all you bruh."

"First of all, what yall ain't gon' do is talk about me like I ain't here! Ole retarded ass niggas!" she huffed looking between the two of us with the exact same facial expression that Kendu had, had just a second before.

"Damn, why I gotta be retarded ma?" he asked and she promptly ignored him turning her attention to me.

"You gon' hook yo' mama up or am I gon' have to get a weed card?" she put her hand on her hip and looked me up and down. As far as I knew her ass didn't indulge in weed of any kind, but then again she had made that weed man comment to me before.

"Yeah we definitely gon' hook yo' mean ass up. It might help yo' attitude problem." Kendu grumbled.

"I ain't mean, I just want you to handle yo' business. Now, I'm your mama, but I'm a woman before anything and if you grown enough to be out here fuckin' without a condom then you grown enough to take care of the baby that comes with it. You already grew up without a father, if this is yo' baby do you really want to put it through the same shit yall went through?" she said and I could tell that she had somewhat put something on his mind. We never talked about Kane Sr. because he wasn't ever a factor in our lives, but there had been times when his absence had been loud. As childish as my brother was, I knew that despite him not wanting kids at the moment he damn sure wouldn't want his kid walking around not knowing who he was. Sighing, he ran a hand down his face.

"Ayite ma, I got you. I'm gon' call her when we leave here." He promised.

"Nah you said that already, call her now." I knew he wasn't expecting her to say that by the look of irritation on his face, but it served his ass right for not telling me about this shit from the beginning. When he took too long to pull out his phone she cleared her throat, prompting him to do what she said, and on some smart shit he showed her the screen as proof that Ashlee was on the other end.

We both watched as he walked off with his phone up to his ear. "I swear somethin' wrong with his ass." she huffed as soon as he was out of ear shot.

"I wonder where he get it from." I just had to throw out there to fuck with her.

"Ayite now, don't get fucked up Kane." She warned with a grin. "how has things been goin' with yo lil' boo?" she nudged my arm and just her bringing up Makiyah instantly had me wanting to see her. We'd gone out a few times so far and each time was better than the last, but I could tell that she was holding herself back when it came to me. From what she'd mentioned of her baby daddy, he'd really fucked her up as far as trust. And even though she hadn't come right out and said it he'd made her insecure as hell, but I was working on that.

"Maaan, slow up, we just cool ma." I told her, even as I felt myself smiling at the thought of her, which my mama peeped right away.

"Just cool my ass. I see you smiling every time somebody bring that girl up. Long as ya'll not tryna make me a grandma too." Smacking her teeth she walked away too, and out of everything she'd mentioned I still had Makiyah heavy on the brain.

A COUPLE HOURS LATER

"Aye, come open the door." I said just as I reached the front of Makiyah's apartment. Already I was anticipating the look on her face when she saw what I had for her. I'd been going out of my way to see her blushing and that gorgeous smile and I was convinced that it was addictive at this point.

"Why didn't you tell me you was comin' Kane? I ain't openin' shit, Iookin' this," despite her attitude I could still hear smiling bashfully through the phone and that had me even more ready to see her face.

"Maaan, come let me in." I didn't even wait for her to answer as I stopped in front of her door and hung up. It took a few seconds, but she eventually opened up for me looking like she was on her way to bed. Even with her hair in a wild ponytail and some oversized sweats on though she looked good enough to enough to eat literally. It'd been a minute since that first dinner date, almost a month to be exact and every time I was around her, I was having a hard time keeping my mind out the gutter. As usual she looked up at me shyly, still not noticing the bag in my hand.

"Heeey Kane." She said sweetly, and I pulled her into a hug. The smell of whatever sweet smelling lotion she was wearing had me tempted to kiss her exposed neck as I held her.

"Sup baby." I could've sworn she shivered when I said that, but just as quickly as the thought crossed my mind she was pulling away and putting space between us. Smirking, I stepped completely inside noting how clean it was for a toddler to be living there. She even had some candles lit that had the whole front smelling like syrup. Some girly ass music was playing and the tv was on but muted so I knew she'd already been in the living room. That was further proven by the half empty glass of wine, notebook and pen sitting on the coffee table.

I went and made myself comfortable on the couch and after a few seconds she joined me, sitting on the farthest end away from me, and I fought not to laugh. "what you was doin'?"

"Ummm, I was just tryna get some writing done." She sighed snatching up her notebook and wine with a creased forehead. She'd told me about wanting to become an author and I thought that shit was cool as fuck. It was a lot of bitches that didn't even want to read a book let alone write one and just the way her eyes lit up when she talked about it showed how passionate she was.

"Yo' hand don't get tired doing it like that?" I nodded towards the notebook, in awe. As far as I knew she hadn't actually started writing anything yet because she didn't have laptop, but to see that she'd taken the initiative and was doing it free-hand just to get started had me feeling even better about my gift.

"Sometimes, but usually when it does I just take a break." Shrugging again she looked off unable to make eye contact with me, so I slid closer and could literally see her breathing pick up.

"Let me see." I reached out and she bucked her eyes, pulling the notebook closer to her chest, but I managed to get it anyway.

"It's not ready yet!" she whined lunging for it, but she couldn't do too much since she was still holding her glass. I took advantage of that, and was able to skim the page looking back at her in humor after seeing that she was in the middle of a sex scene with a nigga named Cain. That look alone had her covering her face in embarrassment as I chuckled and tried to pull her hands away. "Kaaaaane!"

"You talkin' to me or the nigga in this book?" I teased, still trying to wrestle for her to look at me.

"You weren't supposed to read that!" she sat up folding her arms across her chest. She looked like a big ass kid.

"Ayite, Ayite." I told her handing it back to her and her mean ass snatched it back gaining another chuckle out of me. "my bad baby for real. I done got completely sidetracked cause I only came to bring this to you." With her acting like she was mad at my ass now was the perfect time to smooth shit over with my gift. She didn't react immediately when I lifted the Apple bag from the side of the couch, I guess that shit was delayed because a second later she was looking between me and it with wide eyes. I held it out further to her and when she still hadn't taken it I set it in her lap. With her eyes never leaving mine she reached inside and when she pulled out the latest Macbook Air, she pushed that shit right back in there shaking her head profusely.

"I can't take this, it-it's too much."

"You already know I spend my money on what I want." I said lifting her chin so that she was looking at me. "But this right here is an investment in *you*. I believe you can do whatever you put yo' mind to and to prove it I want you to have the tools you need to get started on yo' dream. I just better get a dedication or some shit or I'm suin' yo' ass for using my likeness in that muhfucka." I tried to lighten the mood with a joke, but shorty had tears in her eyes.

"This is the nicest thing anybody's ever done for me." she choked and before I even knew what was happening she was kissing me. Off instinct I lifted her into my lap as the kiss got deeper and she pushed her tongue into my mouth. I'd been wanting to feel her soft ass lips since the first day I'd met her and immediately my dick started to awaken as I let my hands roam her body.

"Mmmmm." She grinded against me moaning. I helped her out of the sweatshirt she was wearing, and was met with her bare breast. Shorty was getting off from just the friction and she threw her head back, breaking our kiss. I immediately attacked her neck, making sure that there was a hickey there before traveling down to her chest. "ssssss Kaaaaane." I'd never heard my name sound so fucking sexy coming off a woman's tongue and my dick got so hard I thought that shit was gonna break. Slipping my hand into the waistband of her sweats, I was met with a whole puddle, no I was met with a fucking lake that's just how wet she was and I groaned lowly.

"Fuuuuck Ky, tell me what you want me to do with this wet ass pussy baby." Her shit was slippery I could barely keep my thumb steady on her clit.

"Ohhhh myyyyy! Right there!" she shrieked squeezing her eyes closed. "Keep doin' thaaaaat!" her body shook as an orgasm finally ripped through her before she dropped her head into my shoulder panting. Or at least I thought she was, it took me a second to realize that she was actually crying and when I went to pull away she covered her face.

"Aye, aye aye. What's wrong baby?" my dick was still on brick underneath her, but I quickly shifted my focus.

"I'm so soooorry. I-we shouldn't be doin' this." She was already trying to remove herself from my lap while I looked on confused as fuck. Covering her chest she looked around for her sweater and found it on the tv stand. She'd already tossed it on and was shoving the Apple bag into my chest by the time I finally unfroze myself and stood up from the couch. "I'm really sorry Kane, I'm just not ready to take it there with you." Her ass pushed me all the way to the door, apologizing and shit incoherently.

"Look, it's cool. I'm not just fuckin' with you to get to know yo' pussy. We can move as slow as you want, but this shit was a gift and I ain't takin' it back." I softened my tone, handing the bag back to her and kissing her forehead, all while my dick was still fighting to be let free. As I walked out to my car I realized that, I wasn't even mad at her. Makiyah was fragile so if it took me some time to get her to trust me then I'd give her that, but I was going to have to find a way to release the sexual frustration my ass was building every time I was around her.

17

MAKIYAH

"Mmmhmm, her ass just as bad as Kya!"

"I swear, like damn bitch can you be more discreet?"

"Her and her cousin snatched them niggas up fast though. Didn't even give a bitch a chance to holla!"

I rolled my eyes at the shady bitches I worked with talking shit within listening distance of me. They obviously thought I wouldn't do shit because of my quiet nature, but they'd soon find out I was just as wild as Dymani. The whole time they were talking I continued to stock up the bar like I didn't hear their miserable asses which only had them sucking their teeth and grunting more. I was trying to focus on the task at hand and not think about the embarrassing shit that happened with Kane the other night. On one hand I felt bad that I'd let things get that far and on the other I like a fool for clamming up on him. I was confused to say the least, and what made it even more confusing was that he hadn't switched up on me after the fact. I thought for sure he'd become an asshole again, but he'd been just as nice as always.

As a woman, it was hard trying to use discernment when it came to niggas. There were times when it was easy to spot warning signs and then there were times when they'd hide that shit until they got what they wanted from you. My mind kept trying to protect me from experiencing the same hurt that I had with Romell, but my heart was ready to let Kane in. It was a constant war going on and I really didn't know what side I should take. On another note, I'd finally broken down and opened the laptop he gave me, and had been typing nonstop. It was that much more special that he'd believed in me enough to go purchase something like that for me. Romell would've never. In fact, he always had something negative to say whenever I mentioned wanting to be an author.

"Bitch, relax yo' face. You over here lookin' like you wanna kill the glasses and shit." Dymani hopped onto the empty barstool in front of me, and like magic the hating hoes disappeared.

"Shut up, this my thinkin' face." I huffed and rolled my eyes before looking her over. Ever since her and Kendu's date her ass had been glowing, and radiating happiness, which I loved for her. I just knew after the whole funeral fiasco she was going to be down for a while, but surprisingly she wasn't and that was probably all because of Kendu. She'd deny that shit if asked, but I knew the truth. Smirking she leaned over the bar so that nobody else would hear.

"Nah, that's yo' coochie thinkin' you a damn fool for not letting Kane up in there." she giggled. "yo' shit gon' close up like an earring hole if you don't use it soon, watch what I say."

"Girl!" I cackled. "You and Du belong together, yall say anything out yall mouth." I peeped the way her eyes lit up at the mention of that nigga, and was going to call her out when heels clicking across the floor brought my attention to the entrance. The same beautiful woman I'd seen with Kane at Yolk was coming our way, and I couldn't help feeling a little insecure as I looked her over. She was dressed from head to toe in designer, and rocking a lace front that literally undetectable to the naked eye. I'd completely forgotten about her, but now that she was in my presence again it was hard not to cop an attitude. I really didn't even know who I was more mad at, Kane for having options that looked the way she did, or myself for leaving him open to those options. Even though I'm sure I was giving her the evil eye, she still smiled upon seeing me and walked over. Straightening up I attempted to match her energy, because the truth was this lady hadn't done shit to me and besides that I was at work.

"Hello welcome to Eclipse. Can I help you?" I greeted her as politely as I could.

"Hey girl, actually I was looking for Kane, he told me to meet him here." Her tone was just as warm as her smile had been and I could tell that under any other circumstances I would like her. Since she was there looking for the nigga I was currently harboring feelings for though I found it hard to control the way my nose turned up.

"Sure, I'll call him down." I forced a smile as Dymani bucked her eyes at me and mumbled something under her breath, but I was already moving over to the phone. A mix of emotions ranging from hurt to jealousy washed over me as the line rang, and when he answered it came out in my tone.

"Hello-."

"Your lil' lady friend that you invited is here." I said tightly, mad that I was even feeling some type of way about it.

"Maki-."

"You better come get her, before I let her know your ass was just at my house tryna fuck!" I hissed lowly, slamming the phone back on the hook and turning around to find her and Dymani engaged in conversation. Instantly my brows dipped at how phony my damn cousin was for fraternizing with this bitch. With narrowed eyes, I cleared my throat, interrupting whatever they were saying. "he'll be right down."

Despite how nasty I knew it came out, she still said thank you, which just irritated me more. Dymani was trying to discreetly shake her head at me, just as Kane made it down the stairs. I watched him with my eyes narrowed to slits, as he kissed ole' girl on the cheek like I wasn't even there.

"What's up Ma?"

"Hey baby." She gushed back and I almost threw up in my mouth. I guess it was a good thing that I had stopped him from fucking me silly that night. Instead of returning to the end of the bar where I'd been when she first got there I stayed where I was, pretending to be busy.

"I see you already met Dymani and Makiyah." I stiffened at the sound of my name and peeked at them through my lashes.

"Yeah, I see you took my advice. She's definitely as thirsty for you as you are for her." She said and my snapped in their direction ready to go off, while her, Kane and Dymani laughed.

"Excuse me!"

"Broooo you trippin' mama ain't nobody thirsty!"

"Shiiiiit, she looked like she was ready to take me down when I came in asking for you. She definitely thirsty, and a lil' crazy too." She pointed out, but I was still stuck on him calling her mama.

"Ahhh look at her face! She definitely thought you was somebody he was messin' with Ms. Regina!" Dymani was quick to add and I fought to straighten out the scowl I felt on my face.

"So..you're not messin' with Kane?" I questioned slowly trying to wrap my mind around her being his mama and not some hoe he was talking to. That had them falling out in another fit of laughter as I took another long look at her. Ms. Regina didn't look like she was old enough to have two grown ass men as sons, but I was suddenly seeing some slight resemblances between them and it had me feeling stupid as hell.

"No honey, him and his brother came out my cooch, and ain't none of us interested in them being back in there!" she cracked making Kane's face ball up.

"Man what the fuck ma, ain't nobody tryna hear 'bout yo' area!" he couldn't even bring himself to say coochie as he shuddered.

"Boy, in case you ain't noticed I got a vagina just like every other woman." She huffed making him look off grumbling and I could tell that a majority if not all of their conversations were just as colorful. Ms. Regina was hilarious and I was glad that I had let any of the shit I'd been thinking slip out of my mouth like I'd wanted to.

"Oh my god, I'm so sorry if I was being rude." I attempted to apologize but she waved me off.

"It's fine, you were actually way nicer than I would've been honey. Mama just got a sixth sense about these things so I could look at you and tell my baby got you open." Winking she took a seat at the bar next to Dymani. "now can you make me something fruity, cause I ain't tryna tour this huge ass building without a drink!" Kane just shook his head as I got the stuff together to mix her up the best Sex on the Beach I could.

When they finally walked off I looked at my cousin with my forehead bunched. "Bitch you could've told me somethin'!" I hissed cleaning up my area again, since the club would be opening soon.

"Shit, I tried to but yo' ass was too busy thinking him and his mama had something going on." She hunched her shoulders, looking like she was trying hard not to laugh.

"Fuck you heffa."

"Don't fuck me, fuck Kane you'll probably like it better!" She cackled like a damn hyena and twerked in her seat. Her ass swore she was on Comic View or some shit, and was still laughing when I threw the towel I'd been cleaning with at her before walking off to the bathroom. "I hope you goin' to take my advice!" She called out to my back and I flipped her the finger over my head.

I just needed a minute to get my feelings back in check and I clearly wouldn't be able to with Dymani's extra ass around. I'd almost just embarrassed myself in front of Kane again by assuming shit and I was almost afraid to face him. He was probably confused as shit. One minute I wasn't trying to elevate what we had going on and the next I was ready to fight his mama cause I thought she was fucking with him. The thing was that I wasn't even sure about my feelings and I didn't want to be rushed into anything. Sighing I looked at myself in the mirror with narrowed eyes.

"Figure out your shit bitch." I grumbled and rolled my eyes when somebody pushed open the door. A bitch couldn't get five minutes to herself in this damn club! I wasn't expecting Kane to be the one rounding the corner though and my breath got caught in my throat. When his gaze landed on me he stopped and leaned against the wall, sizing me up without words. "You know this is the lady's room right?" I finally said and he reached back to lock the door with a smirk.

"I do, but I saw you come in here when I was walking my mama out and thought we needed to talk." I licked my lips, eyes bouncing around the room before landing back on him suddenly nervous. Just because things had seemingly gone back to normal since the night at my house didn't mean I felt in control enough to be around him alone. My body was already responding to him and the intoxicating cologne he always wore.

"About!- About what?" I had to catch myself because my voice was coming out squawky as hell.

"About what we doin'." He cocked his head and closed the distance between us. "I know you don't wanna move too fast cause you're scared I'm gon' do something to hurt you. And it damn sure ain't been long enough for me to prove that I won't, shit I probably couldn't even promise you that. Like I said though, I wanna see where this shit goin' 'cause it's definitely something here baby even my mama see it."

My heart was pounding away in my chest as he cupped my chin with his lips hovering above mine. It would be so easy to just tell him yes, but I'd only just partially pulled myself out of a dark place. The last thing I needed was to get involved with him and set myself back if he did do something to hurt me. At the same time I didn't want Romell to have that power over me anymore. In such a short time Kane had done more for me than my baby daddy ever had. He'd spoken life into my dream and was so different than what I was used to that I realized he should be treated as such. I probably still wasn't ready to give him my body but there wasn't anything wrong with giving him access to me heart.

"So, if I say yes...then what?" I blinked already knowing that I would.

"It's gon' be you and me, fuck everybody else."

18

ROMELL

I wasn't an R&B listening to ass nigga, but I had to cut up the radio as Miguel sang. It was like that nigga knew exactly what the fuck I was dealing with and had written the shit just for me. I'd for damn sure be clowned if anybody in my crew caught me out there in my feelings but that's exactly what I was and I was in them bitches deep! After three months in Miami our shit had taken off and I was touching real paper, more than I'd ever seen in my life. But like the saying goes more money more problems.

As much as I didn't want to admit it I'd fucked up. My mind had been so set on getting the money and the product, I hadn't considered what I'd do when we ran out. We were getting down to the last bit of work we had and we'd been stepping on that shit trying to stretch it until we could actually find a connect. The way shit was going though we were losing more money than we were gaining and that was creating issues for me in the streets and in my own home. The everyday trappers weren't happy about the condition of the work, and they damn sure weren't happy about being out for hours and not making shit. I kept promising them I'd be coming with some new product soon, but that shit was way harder than it seemed. It wasn't like them niggas were advertising on the street that they had weight for sale, and since I didn't have any real ties to the dope game I didn't have any way to get in touch with a supplier. I'd been working on getting a meeting with Ricardo, but that shit was harder than breaking into the White house. He was such a big wig in the game that getting in touch with his ass took different levels of clearance and I hadn't even reached level one.

On top of that Simone wasn't the same at all. The money had quickly gone to her head and all she was good for was eating, sleeping and shopping. She didn't even realize that my pockets were drying up or maybe her ass just didn't give a fuck. At five months pregnant she was self-centered as hell and just overall lazy. If it wasn't for the maid I had coming in everyday, our luxury skyrise would be a nasty ass mess. The job transfer she'd gotten before we left had been wasted, cause her ass hadn't stepped foot in a bank since we'd gotten there unless it was to make a withdrawal. About the only good thing I could say was that she was at least keeping herself together, with weekly trips to the hair and nail salon. The warm weather kept her in little ass shorts and sundresses, both of which had her booty looking juicy as hell, but she never wanted to fuck. Any time I tried to get some pussy she was complaining about her back, or being tired, which led to me getting the shit elsewhere.

I was literally living the same life I had been living with Makiyah, except it was in what some would consider a better setting. The similarities had her and Rj on my mind heavy, and I realized I'd been so caught up in building here that I hadn't even called or sent a text to check on my son. When I did try though, I quickly learned my ass was blocked from everything and didn't have no way of getting in contact with her. Curious, I did some bitch shit and made a fake page. She accepted my friend request within a day and as soon as I was in I started stalking her shit. The Makiyah that I'd left only ever had whiney ass quotes posted or something about our kids, but the first thing that popped up was a picture of her that had me doing a doubletake. She was dressed up, and looked sexy as hell with a caption about a date and despite the shit I'd said to her jealousy shot through me. A Date? Our daughter hadn't even been gone two whole months and she had been going on dates and shit. Getting all dressed up, when she could barely comb her hair for me? I had to know who this nigga was and since she hadn't put a picture of him up, I found myself checking her page daily to catch a glimpse of him. Every day she was posting pictures of her, at work and at home with Rj, and in each one she was looking happier than the last. She clearly wasn't the same lazy, bum I'd left weeks before and I'd just found out why. Shit, I'd already been having a bad day and had fell out with Simone, but it only got worse when I went to my baby mama's page. Right there for the world to see was a picture of her posted up with none other than one of the nigga's who ran GMM. I was sick. As far as I knew she didn't even run in the types of circles that would put her around a nigga like him. I'd made sure of that shit! I should've known the second I'd left that her hoe ass cousin would have her out around all types of niggas. Now she seemed like she was living up to her full potential. Taking care of herself, going out, working. I'd even seen her post about starting her novel and that was some shit I hadn't heard her bring up in a minute.

My ego wouldn't let me accept that I was the reason she'd been so fucked up while we were together. It was no way I could've been her downfall when she'd been mine all this time, holding me back from the shit I deserved out of life or at least I thought. I deserved Makiyah at her best since I'd dealt with her ass at her worst. That nigga had come in and recycled the shit out my sloppy seconds and I couldn't help but wonder if she'd had him around my son. Was it a mistake to leave them? Did I make the right choice between her and Simone?

I'd probably fucked up and handed the next nigga my good thing and I was too selfish for that. Makiyah would always be my bitch and I surmised that if I wanted to I could get her back. It wasn't like that nigga didn't have his choice of bitches to fuck with and even though I knew my baby mama was special, it wasn't no way his ass had a real interest in her. Either he was fucking with her for sex, or his ass was using her to get close to me. Both of those sounded better than him actually giving a fuck about her to me. I could definitely understand him wanting to fuck, because Makiyah had addictive ass pussy, but if he was trying to get information from her about what I had going on then he was wasting his time. I'd been smart enough not to tell her shit about what I'd done or where I was going.

I sat in my new Denali, smoking as I considered my options. I could help her out of whatever she'd gotten mixed up in or could let him find out on his own that she didn't know shit. By the time I finished my blunt and had pulled up to my building, I'd made up my mind what to do.

"Where yo' ass been?" as soon as I stepped foot into our living room the light clicked on and I spotted Simone on the couch, in only a sports bra and some boy shorts. I sighed immediately, feeling too tired to argue with her ass anymore that night.

"I was out making money Simone damn!" I pulled out the wad of bills I'd had on me when I first left and hoped that she believed me. The sight of the money had her eyes lighting up and she came at me with a softer tone.

"I'm sorry baby, this pregnancy just has me so emotional." She whined and tried to struggle to her feet. I started to let her fat ass figure it out on her own, but decided to help her and as soon as she was standing before me she had her hand out. "since your pockets are up, can I have some money for my hair tomorrow?"

"You just got that shit done! You don't need no money for that!" I roared already tired of her and I'd only been back in the house for a few seconds. Truthfully, I didn't know if I was really mad about the money or about what I'd seen on Makiyah's page, but either way she was going to get effects of that shit. As soon as the last word left my mouth though she drew back like I'd slapped her, looking at me through narrowed eyes.

"You don't tell me what I need especially when I been here away from my family and friends for you! The least yo' ass could do is fund my hair and some shopping!" I don't know why but the first thing that came to mind was that Makiyah would've never said no shit like that. As mean as I was to her, she always only ever wanted me and not what I could do for her. While Simone constantly had her hand out. She didn't even see anything wrong with what she'd just said and stood there staring me down like she dared me to argue with her. Smacking my lips, I stuffed my money back in my pocket and left her right there without another word. "Really Romell!" she hollered behind me as I stepped into our bedroom and locked the door. Her ass could sleep in the guest room or the baby's room, but she wasn't going to be sleeping with me...not that night anyway. I ignored her banging on the door and went to take a shower with Makiyah on my mind.

19

KENDU

"Ayite lil' mama, this the last time I'm baby sittin'. You don't be payin' enough!" I fussed as I pretended to rock Armani's pissy ass Baby Alive. She stayed feeding her a bunch of bullshit right before she'd hand her off just so I'd be stuck changing those weird ass diapers. At first I'd save them for her, because I didn't know shit about none of that, but after she chewed me out in baby talk I figured it the fuck out. She looked at me with her little eyebrows knitted together and reached into her purse to hand me a bunch of fake money.

"Pay!" after throwing the bills into my lap, she buttoned the little bag back up and dramatically tossed it over her shoulder, just like her mama always did. "Rock baby, Doo doo!" she scolded and I immediately did as she asked. For as much shit as I talked, she had me wrapped around her little fingers and could make me do whatever she wanted. My guilt had inserted me into her life and now I couldn't see myself not being around her. I was attached like a muhfucka and knew that at this point even if I no longer fucked with Dymani, I'd still want to be involved with her.

"You crazy, she definitely 'bout to go take a nap on yo' ass and gon' want you to still be holding that doll when she get back." Dymani laughed from where she was sitting on the other couch.

"Yeah ayite, this lil' muhfucka gon' be over there with you and I'm gon' be up." I told her dead ass serious making her shrug like she knew better. It was a damn shame that a toddler was running around controlling what we did.

In the last few months I'd gotten comfortable as fuck spending time with the two of them even though I tried to deny it. I'd even fucked around with a few other bitches thinking it would help, but I still found myself stuck up under Dymani's ass. At the moment I could've been making a few moves, but I'd stopped by and ended up eating the lunch she'd made. Now I was half sleepy and half horny so I'd taken up residence on the couch.

My phone started vibrating beside me and I ignored it since it was only Ashlee....again. It seemed like since she'd gotten pregnant all her ass did was call me. I'd done what my mama said and was doing my best to be there for her but the bitch was making it hard. Calling me all hours of the night and shit to bring her odd ass snacks, and whining about her feet swelling like I could do something about it. The further along she got the worse she became and I was just waiting on shorty to pop so I could get a blood test done. Until then I was going to do the bare minimum contrary to what she believed. Her latest issue was planning a baby shower I had no intention on going to, but if she wanted to keep planning that shit with my voicemail then that was on her.

I don't know why but suddenly I was wonder what Dymani looked like big and pregnant. She had the body type that would only have her stomach growing while the rest of her body stayed fairly small. No doubt she'd be pretty as hell and glowing which didn't happen with everybody. Thinking about her pregnant had my dick growing in the joggers I wore and I made no attempt to cover it up.

"Aye, come over here I'm tryna rub on yo' booty and shit." I eyed her thick thighs and licked my lips.

"What?" She looked back with her nose crinkled up.

"I said bring yo' pretty ass over here so I can rub on that fat ass booty." I repeated and she blushed all cute and shit.

"Ain't you supposed to be baby sitting?"

"Maaan this lil' muhfucka sleep, come on." I beckoned her with one hand and set the baby down with the other one.

"Don't get on no freaky shit with my grand baby right here." She plopped down next to me and said but I wasn't paying her ass no attention, I was more focused on the vanilla scent coming off her. I immediately pulled her leg across my lap and squeezed a handful of her ass. "Stooooooop Du."

"Stop what?" I asked never removing my face from the crook of her neck. As usual it wasn't taking much for her to respond and I was pretty sure her pussy was already dripping for me.

"Thaaaaat." Panting she tried to wiggle out of my arms but I wasn't having that unless she was going to wiggle onto my shoulders and put that pussy in my mouth. I was definitely sprung as fuck if I was willing to pleasure her without poking or getting head myself. Whatever shorty was eating had me slurping more pussy than I ever had in my life.

"Ayite, you gon' sit on my face then?" I asked never missing a beat.

"No, you supposed to be babysitting not tryna freak on me." Her limber ass slipped out of my arms and stood up quick as hell.

"I'm tryna eat you not freak you tho baby." I told her licking my lips suggestively just as Armani's little ass came running up the hallway. Already knowing I'd lost my opportunity she stuck her tongue out at me and switched off to the kitchen.

"Doo doo, you let baby falls!" Armani shouted snatching my attention away from her mama's ass and like a trained puppy I picked it up and was rocking again just like Dymani's ass had said.

. . .

EVERY SAVAGE DESERVES A HOOD CHICK

After sitting over there and playing with Amarni for a little bit longer while Dymani's ass hid. I decided it was time to go. Truthfully, Ashlee had still been calling and although I wasn't trying to be bothered with her I figured I'd go see what she wanted since she lived right up the street.

I fucked around and just walked the short distance since I was already on her block. As soon as I stepped through the door she was running down a list of shit she wanted me to grab from the store. Since I really hadn't even wanted to stop over there in the first place,I didn't put up a fight about getting the items on the list. I drove straight to the Walgreens around the corner and drove right back making sure that Dymani ass didn't see me.

"Ashlee! I got yo' shit!" I hollered once I made it back and didn't see her. Since she'd gotten pregnant I hadn't went too far into her shit, not even to see the nursery that she was always trying to convince me to see.

"Can you bring it to me!" Her voice traveled from somewhere in the back and I instantly got irritated, but I remembered what my OG said and decided not to be an asshole. When I found Ashlee she was in her room laid out with the lights off. She had some of those thick ass curtains that blocked out the sun so it was damn near pitch black in that bitch. "Just sit it on the night-stand." She said groggily. I'd been standing in the open doorway fully expecting her to get her ass up until then. The second I was close enough, she had her hands in my sweats.

"Bro what the fuck you-?"

"Shhhh just let me taste it." She whispered with her lips against my dick. Before I could object any further she'd already swallowed it whole and it felt like my legs were locked in place.

"Gaaaawd damn!" It'd been a grip since I'd felt her throat and I hadn't even realized how much I missed that shit. She moaned causing a vibration and massaged my balls with her soft hands. My fucking toes curled in my shoes and I grabbed the back of her head getting more into it. It wasn't long before I was spilling my kids down her throat with my eyes squeezed shut from the sheer pleasure of it all. That good ass feeling only lasted for a few seconds and once my heart rate returned to normal I realized I'd fucked up. Ashlee licked her lips and any of the nut that had spilled onto her chin with a pleases smile on her face.

"Can I feel now since I already tasted it?" She quipped looking up at me with wide eyes. I swear I was telling myself not to go there but it was like a devil and angel on my shoulders. I'd already fucked up, wasn't no point in turning back now.

A FEW DAYS LATER....

I walked through the packed club making sure that everybody was having a good time and shit. With all of the upgrades that we'd come up with it was running way smoother and the money was flowing even more now. If Sean could see the shit now he'd definitely be impressed with it, and even more salty that he couldn't come up with the money to get it back. I'd heard from more than a few people that his drug problem had gotten out of control after we'd taken over and the nigga ended up in jail over a possession. That was better for me since I wouldn't have to kill his ass for trying to come get his shit back. Being a club owner looked good on me and I was considering talking to Kane about opening another spot soon.

I peeped Dymani moving through the room with some bottles headed to one of the VIP sections and instantly thought about pulling her ass up to my office for a quickie, but my phone started going off with a call from Kane. His ass wasn't nowhere but in his damn office, so I detoured and found him standing in front of his desk with a wide ass grin.

"Nigga what yo' ass in here smilin' like the joker for?"

"I got a call from our people in Miami." He said cryptically and my forehead scrunched in confusion.

"Okaaaay so?"

"So, guess who started up an operation down there, but done ran into a drought?" I guess the fact that I still was confused was written on my face because he sighed heavily. "A nigga named Ro." He finally said.

"Ohhh shit!" I'd forgotten all about that nigga with all of the shit we had going on, but the reminder put him right back on my radar. "so what we bouta do?"

"Shiiiit we takin' flight nigga." He shrugged dapping me up.

"Miami here we fuckin' come!"

20

DYMANI

"So Makiyah, I heard you got a birthday comin' up." Ms. Regina said before taking a bite of her food. We were out IHOP having their weekly breakfast and since me and Makiyah had been with the guys, we'd tagged along. Their mama didn't mind at all either because she said she actually liked us, and that was a lot coming from her, because Ms. Regina didn't bite her tongue for nobody.

Makiyah finished the food in her mouth before answering. "Yeah, it's on the twelfth."

"Oooh you a wishy-washy ass libra." Ms. Regina cracked making us all laugh. "Yall got any plans?"

"Ummm I really wasn't-."

"Oh we definitely got plans." Kane interjected sharing a look with his brother. I couldn't help but wonder what those niggas had up their sleeves as Kendu turned and smirked my way. Makiyah had the same confused ass expression as me, so she clearly didn't know either.

"I hope it ain't something I'll need a sitter for Kane because Ms. C-."

"No need for a sitter cause Rj and Armani comin' with us." He shrugged and she grew even more antsy.

"Is it a surprise? Or can I guess?" she asked excitedly damn near bouncing in her.

"It's a surprise, but I might make an exception if you....." without even knowing what he was whispering in her ear I knew it was some nasty shit just from the way she was blushing and I rolled my eyes. They were just as bad as me and Kendu when it came to sex so I wasn't even surprised.

"Nah uh, none of that! You over there being mannish and I'm tryna eat! Shit I'll tell yall, they taking yall to Miami for a week!" Ms. Regina blurted making the guys grumble as me and Makiyah screamed.

"Really? You taking me to Miami?" she squealed grinning so hard I knew her damn cheeks hurt and he nodded with a pleased look while I looked at Kendu for confirmation. It may not have been much to somebody else but we'd never been out of the city before, not even to the Dell's so this shit was big for us.

I instantly pulled Du in for a hug and planted kisses all over his face, not caring that he was still salty that his mama had snitched. "Awww thanks bae! I definitely need to go figure out what I'm packing!"

"Nah baby, we go shopping for trips....well yall can go shopping together cause I damn sure ain't tryna be in no clothing store with yo' ass." Du shocked me further by saying. I was going to for sure throw that ass in a circle for him later.

"I know yall better stop all that screamin' before they try to put our black asses out." Ms. Regina chimed looking around like she wished a nigga would and I cracked the fuck up. I almost didn't even have an appetite anymore after finding out such exciting news. It seemed like it took forever for everybody to finish eating.

After breakfast, the guys sent us shopping with Ms. Regina and their bank cards since they had some other shit to take care of. The fact that there was no limit on the amount we could spend had me even more geeked to hit up the mall, and having a fashionista like Ms. Regina with us made it that much better. I may have enjoyed fashion, but I'd never owned a luxury brand in my life outside of the everyday streetwear shit so I was going to need her help.

She directed us to Michigan avenue and we quickly ended up racked up a bill of ten thousand from just a few items inside of the Gucci store. The cheap bitch that I am was ready to put mine back and so was Makiyah, but we promptly got treated by Ms. Regina for even thinking that.

"Nah uh, them niggas told yall to shop, so shop!" she said sternly before advising the sales associate to ring us up. I couldn't stop myself from smiling as we did the same thing inside of Louis Vuitton and Bloomington's. We'd even gotten a lot of cute things for the kids that they were bound to fuck up.

By the time we were done, I was sure that them niggas were going to kill us for letting their mama bleed their cards and I was almost scared to face Kendu. He'd told me he was going to be coming over after they finished whatever they were doing, but he texted as soon as I'd dropped Makiyah off and said he'd meet me at my crib. That put some pep in my step and I pushed it to try and beat him there, but when I pulled up his truck was already out there. "this sneaky muthafucka." I grumbled realizing that he'd probably been there the whole time.

I stuffed my hands with my bags so I'd only have to make one trip and wobbled up to the door. I managed to get it open and my mouth instantly hit the floor seeing all of the silver and red heart balloons that were hugging the ceiling, as candles lit the room. Before I could call for him, Kendu appeared in the doorway in a pair of black joggers with no shirt and his face twisted irritably.

"That's all you got?" he asked coming over, taking all of the bags out of my hands, and giving me a quick kiss.

"Baby, you did all this?" I circled his neck, holding him in place since his ass was focused on putting the bags away.

"Damn girl yeah." His mean ass grumbled like I was getting on his nerves, and I kissed him again.

"Awwww let me find out I got a sweet thug." I swooned still not letting him go, even as he grunted.

"Brooo don't do that."

"I'm bouta ride yo' dick like a porn star nigga." That had his brow shooting up and a smile forming on his handsome face.

"Oh yeah?" he asked kissing me back.

"Hell yeah." I damn near growled already feeling my panties getting wet.

"Bet." I shrieked as he lifted me up over his shoulder never dropping a single bag and damn near ran to my bedroom.

ONE WEEK LATER.....

It was the day before Makiyah's birthday and we'd just landed in Miami. I was already good and drunk since I hadn't known what to expect on my first flight, and I was glad that the Uber Black was already there waiting for us. We hadn't really planned on doing anything major that day, so I'd dressed in a simple black Balenciaga lounge set, with a jean jacket over it and some matching slides. Kendu's plain ass had just worn a pair of red basketball shorts and a white tee with his signature Jordan's and a snapback pulled down over his eyes. His downplayed look did nothing to stop the female attention that he'd been getting since before we'd even left the city, but I wasn't even tripping. In the last few months my baby had been going above and beyond for me and I knew he was trying. The way he'd manned up with me and Armani had my armor completely down and his ass had forced his way into my heart. So, when bitches were looking I wasn't even pressed at all because I knew his eyes were on me. Besides that I was too drunk to even say shit to anybody and once we got inside of the car I laid my head right on his shoulder.

"Look at yo' drunk ass. You gon' learn not to overdo it." He teased and kissed my forehead softly making my soft ass simper.

"I'm just gon' take a quick nap and then I'll be good to go." I slurred with my eyes closed. I must have fallen into a deep ass sleep though, because I woke up in the bed with him right next to me and it was dark as shit outside. My stomach churned before I could even get my bearings together and I jumped up and ran for the bathroom, glad that the light was on so I could find it. It took me a good ten minutes to empty everything from my stomach and I sat down on the cool tiles to try and relieve the nausea I was feeling.

"You good drunky?" without looking I could tell Kendu wanted to laugh as he padded through the door and knelt down beside me.

"Nooooo. Where's Armani?" I groaned, finally noticing that she wasn't in the bed with us.

"She's in the other room sleeping. Yo' ass been knocked the fuck out for the last five hours. We went to eat and everything." He let me know and I felt even worse for missing our first night out there.

"Ughhhhh, I'm not ever drinkin' again!" my rant was interrupted by another stream of vomit pouring out.

"I'm gon' let you handle this and just call me when you done." Kendu rushed, and damn near ran out. I was in there for another fifteen minutes before I felt well enough to stand up. I realized he'd unpacked for me when I saw my toothbrush on the sink and after I handled my hygiene I stumbled back into the room. Since the threat of throw up was gone he reappeared and helped me back into bed, wrapping his arm around me and I snuggled into his body before falling back to sleep.

The next morning I woke up feeling much better and with my stomach growling like a damn bear. The sun was shining into the room now, so I was finally able to get a good look at it and I was in complete awe. Everything looked so expensive. Stretching I looked out and saw Kendu on the balcony smoking a blunt with his phone against his ear and I wasted no time climbing out of bed and pressing myself into his back.

"Good morning baby." I crooned, planting a few kisses along

his spine and he quickly hung up, pulling me around to the front of him.

"Good morning sexy. You feelin' better?" I nodded looking up at him. Even if I wasn't feeling better the sun shining and light breeze definitely would've aided that. Just from the side I could see that we were high up and the smell of salt water and waves crashing had a bitch feeling superb. "good, good. I gotta go handle some stuff with my brother real quick, but when I get back we can go sight-seeing or shopping whatever you and lil' mama want." He said letting smoke flow out of his mouth as he spoke and I instantly pouted.

"How you gon' leave? I already missed spending a day with you and now you and Kane bouta be gone for god knows how long."

"Let me find out tough ass Dymani, clingy and shit." He smirked deep dimples on full display and that was almost enough to make my attitude disappear...almost.

"Don't do me, I just wanna spend as much time with you as I can....you got me spoiled."

"I know, but it won't take long. This trip was for Makiyah's birthday, but we got some business out here too. I'm gon' knock this shit out though and then you can have all my time."

"Promise?"

"Promise...now go handle that mornin' breath, yo ass bouta burn my chest hairs off!" his rude ass cracked and I sucked my teeth and punched him in the chest lightly.

"Yeah ayite, this the sweetest morning breath you ever smelled nigga!"

"I can't argue facts." He shrugged and dropped a kiss on my lips. "Everything about you sweet baby." This nigga here!

21

KANE

I watched as Makiyah blinked slowly waking up from her sleep and couldn't stop myself from smiling as her eyes landed on the jewelry box next to her. She shot up quickly and looked from the box to me like she wasn't sure it was hers. "Gon' head baby, that's for you. Happy Birthday." I nodded and she picked it up, slowly lifting the lid to reveal a twenty-karat diamond tennis bracelet and matching necklace.

"Awww thank you!" her cry baby ass already had tears streaming down her face and I gently kissed them away.

"You're welcome baby, and it's definitely more where that came from." She set that shit right to the side and jumped into my lap, straddling me. It was shit like that that made me love shorty for real. Most females would've been ready to post a picture for the Gram or put it right on, but not Makiyah. Out of everything I had all she wanted was me and that type of love was hard to find. Kendu would probably roast my ass the fuck out if he knew that I was doing all this and still hadn't hit yet, it just wasn't some shit I would normally do, but Makiyah wasn't the typical girl. I wanted her to trust me with her before she gave herself to me, because no doubt when I finally got in that pussy I wasn't her ass go nowhere.

She was still crying so hard that her body shook and I had to pull back some just to make sure she was straight. "Stop cryin' like this shorty, you got me worried the shit ugly or somethin'." I lied just to lighten the mood and she giggled through her tears.

"Noooo it's beautiful, it's the best thing I've ever got. I'm just not used to being treated so good just for being me. Even when you're not showering me with gifts, you're taking an interest in my son and what he likes, speaking life and power into me and encouraging my dreams. I already knew forever ago, I just wasn't ready to admit it, but I love you and if you don't want to say it-."

"You already know I love yo' lil' ass." I said before she could finish and instead of replying she crashed her lips into mine. Moaning she let me slip my tongue into her mouth as she undid the buttons on the night shirt she was wearing, stripping it away from her body so that her breasts were against me. Once again with little effort she had my dick growing beneath her and I knew she felt it pressing into her opening through my briefs. As much as I didn't want to though I grabbed her hand to stop her when she went to release my shit making her look at me with worried eyes. "you sure you ready for this?"

She nodded without hesitation. "Yeah baby, I am." She confirmed bringing her mouth back to mine and kissing me between each word. That was all I needed to hear. I'd been waiting on the chance to feel her and with one arm wrapped around her back I switched positions, making her lie back. Slowly, I pulled off her shorts and panties before kissing her from the top to the bottom, I even tongue kissed her fucking toes! She sat up on her elbows watching me with a tortured look on her face as I licked up her thighs until I was face to face with her fat ass pussy. Without hesitation I pushed her legs back so that I had access to more of it and damn near moaned my damn self at how good she tasted.

"Ahhhhh!" she was crying already and soaking wet as I alternated between tongue kissing her whole pussy and flicking my tongue over her clit. I held her firmly so that she wouldn't buck her way free, because I didn't intend to stop until she came as many times as her body would allow. I'd waited a long time and I was trying to make up for it. "Mmmmmh Kane baaaaaby! I'm cumming! I'm cumming!" she sniveled tossing her head from side to side and despite the grip I had on her she was still able to lock my head between her thighs in an effort to stop the tongue lashing she was getting.

"Mmm, mmm open up!" I pulled away enough to demand.

"I caaaan't." she whined. "I caaan't cum again!"

"Bet." I took that shit as a challenge and even with her legs locked behind my damn head I was able to latch on to her clit sending her ass into convulsions, but I didn't stop until I tasted her nectar on my tongue.

"Ohhhhh! Ohhhhh my gaaaawd babyyyyyy!" by now she was holding onto my ears for dear life and riding my tongue like a pro until she squirted and wet my whole damn face up. That's when I finally pulled away and slipped out of my briefs wiping her juices off my face. She was curled up on her side by the time she finally stopped riding the wave of that last orgasm but I was just getting started.

Pulling her to the edge of the bed by her foot, I spread her legs and laid between them sucking her breasts while I simultaneously slid between her folds. She was still wet as fuck and I had to stop moving for a few seconds so I wouldn't nut before I even got in the pussy.

"You so fuckin' wet you gon' make me cum quick as hell Ky." I groaned biting into her neck as I finally pushed my way through her walls. Her softly moaning my name and rubbing my back was like some kryptonite shit. Her pussy fit my dick like a glove and even though I hadn't moved yet she was pulling my shit in with her muscles trying to milk me. "Fuuuuck bae!"

"Yesssss, fuck me Kaaaaane!" she panted, biting into my ear as I began to grind into her. With her legs wrapped around my it felt like I was hitting the bottom of her pussy and she cried every time I tapped that g-spot.

"Tell me you love me again, Ky." I demanded forcing her eyes on me as I pulled almost all the way out and slammed back into her.

"Ahhh IIIII looooove yoou! I luuuuh yooou!"

"I love you too shorty." I grinned pecking her lips and speeding up. I could feel myself about to explode, but I couldn't pull out not with the way she was squeezing the life out my dick.

"Ohhhmyyyygaw- right there, right there! I-I'm cummmmming!"

"Fuuuuk me too bae!" I'd barely gotten the words out when my nut shot out coating her walls. It was such a long ass nut, I was still pulsing when I slid out and fell on the bed beside her with my eyes closed. Kendu and I were supposed to be meeting up with our nigga Neal, but I didn't even know if I'd be able to leave without finding my way back inside of Makiyah first.

My dick was already getting hard, and when I felt her warm wet mouth on me, sucking the tip, I knew damn well I was just gonna have to be late.

It took me an hour before Makiyah's ass got tired and fell back to sleep, giving me the opportunity to take a quick shower and meet Kendu in the lobby. He was sitting on one of the couches and when I approached, he looked up at me with his face tight.

"Nigga what the fuck took yo' ass so long?" he huffed, standing to his feet.

"Yo' quick nuttin' ass wouldn't even understand."

"Man fuck you! Ask my bitch, I be fuckin' her into a coma!" he said loudly, making a few of the other people in the lobby look our way in disgust. "Fuck yall lookin' at? I do fuck my girl to sleep!" his crazy ass repeated, completely unfazed by the disapproval. We made our way to the valet, and when they brought the rental Cullinan around, we wasted no time pulling off. Our meeting was with a few of the heavy niggas in Miami because they'd found Ro. I had them hold off on killing that nigga because I wanted to do the honors, especially since it was obvious he didn't have my shit. With the money I was making from the club, and the rest of our supply. I wasn't even tripping about it. Still, this was all about the disrespect and revenge for our dead workers.

"Bro we gotta hit the strip club before we leave for real! I heard the hoes out here got stupid booties!"

"Nigga that's Atlanta." I told him absently, never taking my eyes off of the Miami midday traffic.

"Yo' ass just be wantin' to argue, but I'm not bouta do it." Waving me off, he turned back to the window until we arrived at our destination. We pulled up to the secluded area where a slew of luxury cars all sat parked in a circle like some tv shit. "These extra ass niggas." Kendu scoffed as we exited the car, and they all followed suit. Out of the trunk of the last car, they pulled out somebody with a bloody pillowcase over their head.

"What's up Kane, Kendu." Neal greeted us with handshakes as well as Nip, Trekk, and Zoo, who was holding dude by the arm.

"Sup y'all."

"What's good."

"I appreciate this shit you know I owe you one, and if you ever in my city..." I let my words trail off because they knew what I was saying.

"Bet, but this ain't the nigga Romell. This his right hand." Zoo said, snatching the bag off his head to reveal dudes fucked up face.

"Daaaaamn, yall fucked that nigga up!" Kendu's childish ass whistled behind me as I removed my Glock. Dude blinked rapidly like he didn't know where he was until his eyes landed on each of us, finally stopping on me.

"Wh-what's this about? I'm not even from here." he stuttered, and Zoo slapped his ass upside the head.

"Nigga don't play stupid. Where the fuck Romell's ass at?" once again his eyes bounced around.

"Nah, look at me nigga, I'm the one who's shit you stole!" I barked and he started begging.

"We can't do shit with them pleas boy, yo' ass dyin' either way. At least if you tell us where Romell at, we won't kill yo' whole family." Kendu reasoned with a shrug even though we'd already killed the nigga's pops.

"Okay, okay! You promise to leave my family out this shit?" he asked looking up at me reluctantly.

"I ain't promising another nigga shit, but I do give you my word." I was already getting tired of this nigga. It was easier to get him to rat out his boy, but it wasn't mandatory.

"Ayite....I don't know where he at exactly, but he said he was goin' to look for his baby mama. I guess she's visiting Miami for her birthday and staying at the Ritz. Her name Makiyah, he gon' be where ever she at." He said dropping a bomb on me. Without speaking, I emptied my clip in his ass just for being the one to deliver that shit.

"Nigga was he talkin' bout yo' bitch?" Kendu quizzed, looking confused despite how clear everything was at the moment for me.

"Aye, we gotta go. I know where the other nigga at." I hardly paused long enough to say as I hopped back in my whip, hoping to catch up with Makiyah. I should've known some shit wasn't right, and I felt betrayed like a muthafucka. Kendu was talking, but I barely heard anything his ass was saying as thoughts of killing Makiyah's ass ran wild in my head. Whether she was involved or not, I was going to kill both their asses.

22

MAKIYAH

I limped over to the couch where Dymani and Armani were waiting for me and RJ with a silly ass grin on my face. People probably would've thought my ass was crazy with the way my face was stretched, but I didn't even care. I was finally in a space where I could be vulnerable and admit I was in love with a nigga who meant me no harm. The feeling was so new and special that I just couldn't stop it from showing on my face and it was damn sure evident in my walk.

Dymani turned around right before we reached the seating area, lowered her sunglasses, and eyed me with a grin. I should've known her ass would know, but what I wasn't prepared for was for the bitch to start clapping. Seeing her made both Rj and Armani start clapping and cheering without even knowing what they were happy for.

"That's right y'all yayyyy!" she egged them on.

"Why we clap?" Armani finally said when I guess her arms got tired, and I gave Dymani a warning look.

"Because it's cousin Ky's birthday, and she looks like she gave up that cake, cake, cake, cake, cake, cake!" she sang and started clapping to the beat.

"Uh uh bitch stop!" I cackled.

"I bet he put his name on it!" she continued, and the kids looked between us confused.

"My name?" RJ asked pointing at himself. "I the boy, so my name?"

"Yeah baby, she's talking about me putting your name on my cake cause I love you." I gave Dymani a look that could kill while she laughed completely unbothered by possibly ruining the kid's innocence.

"Yaaaaay! I get my name on the cake!"

"Can my name be on a cake?" Armani asked and joined Rj cheering when I nodded that she could.

"Look what you done started bitch!" I pinched Dymani's arm, and she pinched my ass right back.

"I ain't did shit. It looks like Kane did it all. Keep yo' hands to yo' self tho bitch before I give you these birthday licks I been saving up all year." She quipped, raising her hand high like she was about to slap the shit out of me.

"Anyway, y'all ready to swim?" I flipped her off and turned to the kids.

"Yaaaaay!"

"I gotta pee!" Rj held his privates and looked up at me making a face.

"Rj I told you to pee upstairs!" I fussed rolling my eyes.

"It's cool cause I know Armani ass probably gotta go too." Dymani dismissed, but Armani quickly shook her head.

"No I don't! I wanna swim!"

"Girl, don't play with me. I'll whoop yo' lil' ass in here!"

"Y'all go ahead, we'll just catch up." I told her, waving when she still hadn't moved. "Gon' hoe, I'm a big girl." Since she still was standing there looking at me through squinty eyes, I went ahead and walked off on her ass. There was a bathroom right in the lobby and led RJ over to it. After helping him into the stall, I stood in front of the mirror, snapping a few pictures. He finished quickly, and I helped him wash his hands and dry them before we headed to the door.

"You ready to swim now?" I asked, looking down at him as we walked hand in hand.

"Yeah!"

"Good and then maybe Kane will be back soon." I hoped because I was already missing him, and it had barely been an hour. He told me he had a surprise for me, and I hoped it was a romantic night alone because I loved RJ, but he was definitely going to be cockblocking.

"Yaaaaay Daddy!" hearing him call Kane daddy had me stuck for a second as he tried to wrestle his hand out of mine. "Daddy!" this time he pointed, and I looked up to see none other than Romell standing outside the bathroom door with a gun at his side. I was so damn shocked to see him that my grip loosened on RJ, and he ran right over to him, hugging his legs.

"Long time no see baby."

TO BE CONTINUED.....

ALSO BY J. DOMINQUE

Made in the USA
Columbia, SC
26 April 2025

57182552R00083